■ □ ■ □ ■

PELTSE

and

PENTAMERON

Writings from an Unbound Europe

■ □ ■ □ ■

VOLODYMYR DIBROVA

PELTSE

and

PENTAMERON

Translated by Halyna Hryn

Foreword by Askold Melnyczuk

NORTHWESTERN UNIVERSITY PRESS

EVANSTON, ILLINOIS

Northwestern University Press
Evanston, Illinois 60208-4210

Peltse originally published in Ukrainian in the collection *Pisni Bitlz*
by Alternatyva, Kiev. Copyright © 1991 by Volodymyr Dibrova.
Pentameron originally published in Ukrainian in the journal *Sučasnist,*
January 1994 and February 1994. English translation and foreword copy-
right © 1996 by Northwestern University Press. Published 1996.
All rights reserved.

Printed in the United States of America

ISBN 0-8101-1219-1 (CLOTH)
ISBN 0-8101-1237-X (PAPER)

Library of Congress Cataloging-in-Publication Data

Dibrova, Volodymyr.
    Peltse ; and, Pentameron / Volodymyr Dibrova ; translated by
Halyna Hryn ; foreword by Askold Melnyczuk.
        p.   cm. — (Writings from an unbound Europe)
    ISBN 0-8101-1219-1 (cloth : alk. paper). — ISBN 0-8101-1237-X
(pbk. : alk. paper)
    1. Dibrova, Volodymyr—Translations into English. 1. Hryn,
Halyna. 11. Melnyczuk, Askold. 111. Dibrova, Volodymyr.
Pentameron. 1V. Title. V. Title: Pentameron. VI. Series.
PG3949.14.I27A25 1996
891.7'933—dc20   96-27239
                                                                      CIP

The paper used in this publication meets the minimum requirements of
the American National Standard for Information Sciences—Permanence
of Paper for Printed Library Materials, ANSI Z39.48-1984

■ □ ■ □ ■

CONTENTS

■ □ ■ □ ■
ACKNOWLEDGMENTS

My greatest debt is to the author Volodymyr Dibrova, who fielded every possible question about this text at least twice and whose superb knowledge of English ensured an accurate reading. It was a rare privilege to work with him, and I learned much about the art of translation. My thanks also go out to the many friends and relatives whom I consulted on questions regarding knitting, planing floors, oil painting, the Old Testament, the New Age, etc. David Arnason and Roman Koropeckyj commented on the translation. I am especially grateful to Askold Melnyczuk for his careful reading of the manuscript and generous advice. Susan Harris and Ellen Feldman were everything one could hope for as editors: supportive, kind, and eternally patient. The Harvard Ukrainian Research Institute provided technical support. This project was funded in part by a grant from the Ukrainian Canadian Foundation of Taras Shevchenko.

Peltse (1984) and *Pentameron* (1974–93) is the first published volume in English translation of a new vibrant literature emerging from an unbound Ukraine. It has been wonderful to play a part in that process.

Halyna Hryn

■ □ ■ □ ■

NEWS FROM
LENNON SQUARE

Volodymyr Dibrova, Novelist

ASKOLD MELNYCZUK

I

As a boy I read *Robinson Crusoe* and *Don Quixote* in Ukrainian. Other classics of the Western canon came similarly vested. Ukrainian appeared a marvelously supple language, as deft at raising up Homeric shadows as it was at bringing into focus medieval Spain, rural Sweden, or Edwardian England.

Gradually my reading life developed a parallel track in English: *David Copperfield*, I'm happy to say, came to me in the original. By the time I discovered American poetry, via Whitman, Ginsberg, and Ferlinghetti, I'd become monolingual again.

For a while, though, the tracks ran together. I encountered Dickinson, Burns, and O'Neill alongside Franko, Shevchenko, and Ukrainka. That the names will mean nothing to most readers has always seemed to me a pity, as well as the cause of some frustration. For years I longed to find someone with whom to compare the impressionism of Ford Madox Ford against that of Mykhaylo Kotsiubynsky or the lapidary lyricism of Ivan Franko to that of his contemporary

William Butler Yeats—that is, someone who came to the table from the Anglophone side of the room.

II

There are many reasons why such conversations haven't taken place. Though Ukrainian literature is centuries old, over the last two hundred years the language has been consistently repressed by Russia. Writing in Ukrainian has been an offense punishable by execution or exile. During the seventy-year reign of the Bolsheviks, hundreds of Ukrainian writers were murdered or died in prison: the first, Hryhory Chuprynka, was executed in 1921; the last, Vasyl Stus, died in 1985 in a Siberian camp. Russia's control over its former colony was thorough. When, in 1991, Ukraine declared itself independent, the country had not a single paper mill within its borders.

Meanwhile, the West learned about the literary world of the East from émigrés, refugees, and visitors. The most prominent, wealthiest, and best connected by far have been Russians. Writers, from Vladimir Nabokov to Aleksandr Solzhenitsyn to Yevgeny Yevtushenko, found audiences eager to hear about the other empire. They themselves apparently knew little about life in the colonies. Unlike their Western counterparts, however, Russian writers didn't sound racked by guilt at their relatively privileged status—indeed, the written record suggests a callous disregard at best.

The most gifted were often those most blinded by national prejudices. In his book on Gogol, Vladimir Nabokov encouraged the misperception that Ukrainian literature dealt exclusively with peasant life. In fact, a large percentage of the best prose from the turn of the century focused on middle-class manners.

Literary Ukraine shares roots with Russia: both consider the twelfth-century epic *Song of Igor's Campaign* the cornerstone of their tradition. And both have claims on the man out of whose overcoat Russians say their literature tumbled: Nikolai Gogol. I haven't the space or the expertise to rehearse the merits of the two cases. Let them remain the subjects of debate for professional Slavicists. Certainly Volodymyr Dibrova's comic genius reflects hereditary traces of Gogol in the sentence stream.

III

Volodymyr Dibrova has been called the best prose writer in Ukraine. He himself gave the lie to that statement by moving to Pennsylvania. Whether or not he is the finest prose writer on the banks of the Susquehanna, he is certainly an important addition to the international cast assembled within the borders of the last of the great Western empires.

Born in 1951, Volodymyr Dibrova is a cultural hitchhiker—a man of letters, he is also very much a child of the sixties. After doing a dissertation on Flann O'Brien and folk culture, he wrote a story sequence titled *The Beatles' Song Book,* which among other things underscored how thoroughly Western popular culture had penetrated urban intellectual circles behind the Iron Curtain. His published articles have introduced twentieth-century French drama and contemporary Scottish poetry to Ukrainian readers. He has translated Ionesco, Hardy, Thoreau, and Eliot, and he's gone the other way, too, carrying Ukrainian poets into the *Edinburgh Review.* A few years ago he received a major award for his translation of Samuel Beckett's intricate novel *Watt.*

Dibrova has been a college professor, a journalist, and unemployed. In the late eighties, he worked as Washington correspondent for the Ukrainian independence movement's newspaper. His creative work includes plays, stories, and the two short novels offered here, *Peltse* and *Pentameron.*

Peltse is a comic, brilliantly inventive portrait of the formation of an average Soviet bureaucrat. Anyone wondering how I (or Dibrova) can get away with calling fifty pages a novel might ask themselves why Beckett claimed the same for a piece that's seven pages long. A novel does not live by pages alone; it is defined by the distance a writer can travel across a sentence. Today, a laser inscribes the whole of the *Nuremberg Chronicles,* with their 1800-plus woodcuts and maps, on the head of a pin—and writers have learned similar techniques of compression.

Dibrova has presented us with a complete and deliciously satisfying narrative. The novel opens with a device I believe Elias Canetti pioneered in *Auto Da Fe:* the reader begins by watching a character in action; the field then shifts to the character's mind; suddenly we lose track of where reality ends and fantasy starts: did Peltse really deliver that speech or not? Abruptly the narrator yanks us back to the present, and we realize we'd been swept up in the rampaging hallucinations of a character's wishes and projections. It is a cinematic device that works better on the page than in the movies. The rest of the story develops with the sort of narrative playfulness which, in the English novel, has its roots in the deliberate misdirections of *Tristram Shandy.*

A day in the life of five office workers in a Soviet scientific research institute, *Pentameron* transcends its premise through Dibrova's wit, technical cunning, and the sheer velocity of the exchanges between characters. Written between 1974 and 1993, it is set in the seventies, during what was known as "the period of stagnation," when the counterproductivity of Soviet life had peaked—or, rather, bottomed out. While the absurdity of the atmosphere breathed by the characters has an Eastern European flavor recognizable to readers of Kundera and Gombrowicz, a similar note has been present in American fiction from Melville's Bartleby to the postwar worlds created by Don DeLillo and Robert Coover, both of whom have reflected the stories of mass man swept up by the newly unleashed technological forces reshaping our world.

Dibrova's fictions propose that absurd situations arise if people are inappropriately employed. When bureaucracies fail to note the unique qualities, as well as the value, of their constituent members, when they do not take the time to discover the best use of their human capital, the result is an atmosphere of despair leavened only by the victims' own sense of the ridiculous.

Like Gogol, Dibrova satirizes the ways institutions limit and distort individuals. He also suggests that people who create these systems cripple themselves. As collaborative enterprises, institutions are meant to offer individuals security while serving as vehicles for social and cultural continuity. Too often they erode an individual's sense of his own power and worth, and nurture his insecurity. Fear is freedom's greatest enemy. It's fear of failure that keeps the office workers in *Pentameron* from pursuing their passions and fear that compels Peltse into his first public lie. And while Dibrova satirizes singularly Soviet sins, the rest of us also feel a salubrious sting.

The appearance of these novels constitutes the first Ukrainian fiction published by a major U.S. house since 1960. That year, the Philosophical Library brought out a volume of Mykola Khvylovy's stories—haunting tales about the early days of the Soviet experiment, expertly rendered by George Luckyj. As the muses—and Dibrova's lucky stars—would have it, his translator, Halyna Hryn, was a student of Luckyj's. Both have done their exemplary work with artful brio.

Now that the floodgates have been opened, the torrent dammed up behind Dibrova should rush out with tidal force, so that by the time we get our bearings we'll be faced with a "new" body of literature whose depths we might try plumbing together. Having been closed for so long, the sluices may not stay open forever. Anyway, it's natural that one should worry over such things.

PELTSE

■ □ ■ □ ■

1. The Carafe

WHEN PELTSE WAS FIVE HE HAD A VISION OR WHAT IS
sometimes defined as an epiphany. His family had gone to
visit relatives. Naturally there were other children there, and
while the adults wined and dined, the children raised havoc
and, running around the table, overturned the carafe. The
carafe fell and broke into pieces.

It was unclear who initiated the ruckus—they had all
horsed around equally, except that it was Peltse and no one
else who, attempting to give little Vova a good hard shove,
grabbed him by the collar of his sailor suit. Vova spun around,
and Peltse's hand struck the flowers that, for lack of a more
appropriate vessel, were thrust into a carafe. The flowers fell
over, water flooded across the tablecloth, the carafe bounced,
and with a hop, skip, and jump passed into nonbeing.

Any one of the children could have found him- or herself
in Peltse's position. Tania once broke a telephone, Olezhka
swallowed some ink, Tamara was an incessant whiner, Vova
would one day be expelled from the university, Alik would
dump his third wife, and as for Angela, her wanton ways
were already becoming obvious.

While breaking a carafe is not the worst crime in the
world, it must also be recognized that Aunt Ada had serious
grounds for her wrath.

"Who did this?" she asked, rushing into the room at the sound of broken glass. At that moment Peltse was sure that it was he, because his hand still smarted from the thorns; had that hand possessed the sense of smell, it could have testified that the flowers, bought at the corner store, were not particularly fresh. But Aunt Ada cast such a murderous glare at the little pond sparkling with crystal boats that Peltse changed his mind and thought, "Perhaps it was not I after all, but Vova, for instance, or Angela, to be exact."

And it was at this point that he was seized by a vision, and he saw before him his entire life, as happens only to mountaineers falling off a steep cliff.

More than a single life—a host of lives that glittered with endless possibilities, depending on point of view and, moreover, on choices made.

First he saw himself as a five-year-old, face to face with the furious Aunt Ada. He is taking the resolute step, saying, "I broke the carafe."

His dad pokes his head out of the living room, face redder than usual, raises his meager eyebrows, and says, "Crystal! You scoundrel! Just wait until I . . . "

"No, no, no!" thinks Peltse, and switches into another life, where Aunt Ada, finding no culprit, forces her son Vova to pick up the slivers of glass. And in the meantime, Peltse, having breezed through a number of carefree years, is passionately kissing someone in the park.

Is it Lida? Marusia? Dusia?

"It's like a trip to Fairyland," thinks Peltse. "Disneyland. Like 'Peter Rabbit Meets Dusia the Squirrel.'"

Saccharine music plays as storybook creatures—jackals, hyenas, weasels—step onto the garden path and begin to approach the squirrel. The filmstrip breaks; the audience whistles, stomps its feet, and boos; the projectionist hesitates: which reel comes next? In one of them, the fatally wounded rabbit desperately kicks at the brutes with his hind legs, but falls, knocked off his feet.

"No, not that one, put on another," Peltse shouts at the projectionist. "The one where an agile rabbit dodges between the squirrel and the beasts, into the bushes, a rustle in the grass, a fish under water, away, away, off the screen and into another life, where Mom, having noticed Peltse's hair standing on end, puts the book aside and says, 'Don't be afraid, it's only a fairy tale.'"

"In other words," he asks, "a fairy tale is a lie?"

Mother smiles gently, parts her lips to answer, and Peltse sees two lives simultaneously. In one of them his mother says: "Don't worry, a fairy tale is make-believe." In another she says: "Don't worry, a fairy tale can't lie."

Peltse chooses the first, because there, a little while later, youngsters savor a bottle of wine in a dimly lit stairwell. They stand in a circle, pass the bottle around, one of them reads aloud something subversively liberal. The sweet wine allows Peltse to achieve a state of hitherto-unknown inspiration, and he anxiously taps his foot. The boys are denouncing somebody, they unanimously aspire toward something new and just, something that must come not tomorrow but today, if only all people would come together.

"They," proclaims Peltse, "can't help but join us, 'cause we strive for justice!"

"Justice," the rest of the gang joins in, "and happiness for all!"

"Who, exactly," asks a sober voice in the next scene, "gave you this book?" This unmovable man is looking at Peltse as though he already knows everything, and even if he doesn't, he will undoubtedly extract it from the others.

"Well?" says the man, and this is a sure sign that a fork in the road is just ahead. Indeed it is. One road leads Peltse into a basement where he sits long-haired, armed with a guitar, full of passionate words, in front of a bottle of wine and a tin of canned fish. The basement has two exits: the first to a cold damp room without furniture or wine; the second to a similar basement, but with wine and a slovenly cohabitant, who is about to bestow upon him a quite curable but long-neglected communicable disease.

The other road, having wound its way around the prickly exclamation "well?" carries him out onto a small town square, where a crowd of nearly five hundred has gathered on a frosty morning to hear his, Peltse's, commands.

"Flags?" he asks.

"All distributed," answers his deputy, dressed in a similar outfit.

"Balloons?"

"Them, too."

"And have you checked the drivers? Still sober?"

"Each and every one."

"Well, let's get going then."

The deputy gives a signal and the district brass band contaminates the crisp air with upbeat, earnest dissonances.

While the festive column, with Peltse at its head, marches along the main street, from the place where a church once stood to the place where there used to be another, two mustached artists come through the marketplace gates.

"Who are those bastards?" wonders Peltse. "Not from these parts, obviously. What the hell are they doing here?"

Curiously enough, this pair is also present in a parallel life where Peltse, a farmer in tall rubber boots, is dragging oak logs from the river. It's November, after all, the water level has fallen, and while others are pissing their time away on parades you can pick up plenty of good wood to mend a fence, perhaps, or for the fire.

He sees the column, its leader, the two artists descending toward the river, and thinks, "Who are those wayfarers?"

"How are you doing?" they say to him.

"Fine, what about yourselves?" he answers.

"Must be strangers," he assumes, starts up a conversation, and invites them over to his place for a quick drink.

"They can manage without the drink," decides the other

Peltse, and returns to the life where, to the blare of a brass band, he stands at the head of his district.

In that life he is summoned by Kapsho, who slams an ashtray down on the table and asks why he, Peltse, is constantly opposing his, Kapsho's, orders.

In the deafening silence that follows, only Kapsho's heavy breathing and the rustle of his silk imperial toga can be heard.

Peltse, clad in a grayish fourteen-ruble jacket, stands dumbstruck, hypnotized by the saliva dripping down the fangs of his master's two Dobermans. The dogs let the sticky mucus extend almost to the carpet, and then in one quick slurp suck it back into their gaping jowls.

"And do you un-derr-stand," asks Kapsho in a thick, indestructible accent, "that you may never ever walk out of this room?"

"If I never ever walk out of this room," says Peltse, his voice brimming with dignity, "all decent people of the planet will know about it right away."

The second variant: "All radio, TV, and power stations of the West."

The third variant: "All in whose bodies protoplasm stirs."

All hell breaks loose.

The first variant: The dogs tear Peltse to pieces.

The second variant: Peltse is squeezed sheet-thin by a huge steamroller.

The third variant: Peltse is sliced in half by a laser beam.

"Back!" Peltse jumps out of the way. "Back to another life!"

"And do you un-derr-stand," asks Kapsho in a thick, indestructible accent . . .

"No," Peltse falls to his knees on the carpet gently, so as not to disturb the dogs, "I mean, yes, but you have been misinformed. First, I did this and not that, and second . . . "

Kapsho realizes that it was not Peltse but the rest of his subordinates who flagrantly lied to his fatherly face, and, before dying, he gives orders to do such and such, and names Peltse his sole successor.

At this point the revelation is cut short.

Peltse's last glimpse is of an immense monument to himself (in the form of the immortal carafe) falling off the highest mountain and smashing into tiny particles.

"Who did this?" the ominous voice of Aunt Ada reaches him. "Confess, before it's too late."

"Not me," say Vova, Tania, Olezhka, Tamara, Alik, and Angela.

"Not me," says Peltse.

2. *The Name*

THEY ALWAYS CALLED PELTSE NAMES. DOUGHBOY, PRETZEL, Pukeface, and even Edison. The reason for this was not so much his appearance or character as his name.

"Paltsov?" they would ask at the day care center.

"Peltse," his mother would answer, turning a deep shade of red.

"What was that?" the schoolteacher asks. "Zeltser?"

"Peltse," responds the new boy, clenching his fists.

"Okay, okay, Skeltser." The elementary school educator is a little deaf. "There are all sorts of names around these days. Fokin, Pisarenko, Zashytko. Go sit down beside Askolduk."

"Peltser-Skeltser, Alka-Seltzer," chant the heartless brats. "Shit his panties, couldn't help it."

"It's feces," the teacher corrects them absentmindedly.

Peltse loathed his name, and when forced to introduce himself he did so loudly, accentuating each syllable, staccatolike.

"Pel-tse. Peter, Electricity, Louise, Titanic, Saturn, Edison."

"So are you Peltse or Edison? Want to change your name,

do you? How about if you wait another two years? We've known you as Peltse for three years already, you're Peltse in all the registers, and now the diploma's supposed to go to an Edison?"

The students howled. The lecturer, who conducted seminars in philosophy, had a habit of protruding his belly and making his double chin triple after a successful joke.

Peltse asked his parents whether their unusual surname had a particular meaning, but his mother (née Kokakovska) didn't like her married name and, besides, was afraid of her husband. His father's roots, on the other hand, reached deep into postrevolutionary reform schools, where all trace of them disappeared.

"I must find out. What if it's an aristocratic name?" mused the young Peltse, wrapped snugly in his blanket. "A nobleman, cast on treacherous waters, at the mercy of alien gods. Maybe the name comes from a rare species of plant?"

In the encyclopedia he came across a politician with a similar name, born in the Baltics. When Peltse was sent there as a young professional for refresher courses, he decided to approach his Baltic female colleagues in the dorm next door to try and sort out this issue.

"May I help you?" asked the tall blond who opened the door.

"Well . . . I . . . actually . . . I'd like to see . . . "

"Da-da-da?" She uttered a three-syllable name that Peltse could only have reproduced on a tenth try had it been written on the blackboard in capital letters.

"Yes, please."

"Da-da-da is not in."

"Will she be back soon?"

"I don't know."

"You see . . . I'm actually . . . There's something I must discuss . . . "

"With Da-da-da? Are you her . . . "

"Oh, no, no, by no means. I don't want you to think . . . "

"Was she expecting you?"

"Uh, not really . . . "

"Well, in that case . . . I'm sorry, but . . . "

"Maybe you can help me!"

"Me? What is it?"

"I'll explain everything. Please!"

"Well, as long as . . . All right, come in."

The room was small and tidy. There was nothing cluttering the floor or the beds or the table. There were flowers on the windowsill.

"What can I do for you?"

Peltse noticed a bottle of white wine and some oranges. Is she waiting for somebody?

"There's a word I'd like to ask you about."

"A word?"

"A name, to be precise. I mean, its origin, etymology . . . You see, in the encyclopedia, I came across . . . "

"Which word?"

"Peltse."

The woman stifled a laugh.

"Oh, it's not a word. It's the name of one of our local hacks that we used to have a nickname for . . . "

"A nickname?!"

"Oh, not like that, please don't get me wrong."

"What did you nickname him?"

"Well, he was one of our prominent . . . it's hard for me to even . . . "

"Oh, tell me, please . . . "

"But . . . What's it to you? And anyway . . . "

"I'll be as silent as the grave."

"Okay, we used to call him Da-da-da-da-da-da-da."

She spoke a word that Peltse would only have been able to repeat after a week of intensive drilling.

"But what does it mean?"

"Well, I can't give you the exact . . . "

"Doughboy?"

"No."

"Pretzel?"

"No."

"Pukeface, maybe?"

"No, vomit in our language is da-da-da-da."

"But what about *peltse?*"

"Why on earth are you . . . "

"Because I'm . . . "

"Something serious?"

"Yes, very. It's got to do with gambling. Very desperate bunch. If, God forbid, I don't find out what *peltse* means by tomorrow, they'll get me . . . "

"My God!"

"And you, too."

"Jesus-Mary-Joseph!" The woman dashed for the door.

"Where are you going?" Peltse called after her in alarm. "I was only kidding."

The woman stopped.

"It was a joke. Just tell me what the word you used to call Peltse means, and I'll be off."

The woman hesitated.

"A four-letter word?"

"No."

"Biological substance?"

"No. Just something like 'you're an asshole,' you know."

"Why is that?!"

"I don't mean you, I mean Peltse."

"But I am . . . "

"You?!"

"Oh, no, no, not me, certainly not. I'm Peter, Electricity, Louise . . . "

"Louise? But you're a man?!"

"Never mind. In other words, you claim that Peltse, if properly translated, means asshole?"

"No, that was only his nickname."

"But *peltse,* what does the word itself mean?"

"I don't know."

"What do you mean you don't know? Every word means something. Take Ivanov, for example. That's the son of Ivan. Or Maryna Askolduk. She's Askolduk's daughter. Or . . . Take any name you like. What's your last name?"

"What if you lock the door, run to the balcony, and holler until the police come?"

"What for?'

"To have them all arrested."

"It won't help."

"What if we give them money?"

"Is that your wine?"

The woman ran to the kitchen and brought back a corkscrew and wineglass. While she tiptoed around the room and peeked out of the windows, hoping to catch sight of a police cruiser, Peltse managed to crumble the cork and had to push what was left of it into the bottle. He gulped down half the contents and remembered how as a child he used to wake up in the middle of the night and wonder:

"Am I really Peltse? It can't be true. I'm so small, so cuddly, and Peltse is huge, like that wardrobe, and as mysterious as those things my parents keep hiding in the drawers. Will I really pass the fourth, the sixth, the twelfth grade, grow up to be as big as this name and eventually become a wardrobe myself? Maybe I'm not Peltse at all but simply Me?"

"It's a bloody mystery," he sighed bitterly, and finished the bottle.

"Beg your pardon?" The woman didn't understand.

"Balt yokels," Peltse thought to himself. "And I could have been their lord . . . "

A key turned the lock and somebody opened the door.

"Da-da-da!" The woman sprang to her feet and rushed toward her, scattering handfuls of clear, bell-like, yet completely incomprehensible syllables along the way.

3. According to Dr. Levitov

ONCE, IN A FIT OF EXTREME AGITATION, PELTSE SLAMMED the door and nearly broke his finger.

In such cases Dr. Levitov recommends taking a shower or, after a few warm-ups, going for a swim in a natural body of water. The shower wasn't working, which, incidentally, was the reason Peltse's parents began yelling at him in the first place. And he was unaccustomed to swimming in the river in October. Had he gotten his hands on Dr. Levitov's manual, say, in early spring, he would have certainly worked his way through section A (general fitness) by this time and have been well equipped to deal with the situation.

"If a river, sea, or lake is not to be found in your town, village, hamlet, or railroad junction," wrote Dr. Levitov, "then you are to jog."

Peltse hit the road. Nervous excitation, as predicted by Dr. Levitov, rolled huffing and puffing down Peltse's muscles, rising to the skin surface in the form of sweat. But no sooner did Peltse reach the boulevard than he ran right into a pedestrian.

"Hey!" said the pedestrian, for it was none other than Paltsiuk, Peltse's former classmate. Once, during recess, he had plowed Peltse in the mouth with his fist.

"Looking for trouble?" Paltsiuk had asked then. Peltse was about to say that most likely it was Paltsiuk who was looking for trouble, but at that moment he felt as if he had suddenly sunk his teeth into something salty and wet.

"Hi!" said Peltse. He now knew how to behave in such cases, because Dr. Levitov devoted a separate chapter to them.

Suppose a hoodlum approaches you and asks for a light. You are to step aside inconspicuously in order to divert him from his aggressive course and inquire about something utterly irrelevant and absurd.

"Running, huh?" asked Paltsiuk.

And when the hoodlum subsequently lets down his

guard, strike him in his most vulnerable points. Point A—throat, point B—neck, point C—diaphragm.

"How's it going?" asked Paltsiuk.

"Fine," answered Peltse.

Paltsiuk was the biggest thug in the class. When he got back from the army he sold donuts on the street, then worked in a bottle redemption center, and was now loading and unloading trucks in the back of the grocery store. Peltse often saw him there in his worn-out fatigues, either pushing a dolly or smoking and spitting on the sidewalk.

"Why don't you ever stop by?" Paltsiuk asked.

Peltse had never visited Paltsiuk in his life and now, just to be on the safe side, adopted the stance recommended by Dr. Levitov when he recounted the story about the Japanese tourist and five drunken sailors.

"Been busy lately," he lied.

"Me, too," said Paltsiuk, and before Peltse had a chance to recall the next step suggested by Levitov, Paltsiuk grabbed him by the shoulders and shoved his huge mouth up against Peltse's nose.

"Wanna drink?"

Peltse went into a coughing fit.

"You sick?" asked Paltsiuk. "I got medicine."

He thumped his briefcase against Peltse's legs, and something inside it clinked. Peltse forgot all about Levitov's suggestions and thought only of how to get away.

"I'm in a hurry," he said dryly.

"Me, too," Paltsiuk slobbered all over his ear. "But are we alcoholics or something to booze up alone? By the way, I saw that jerk the other day, what's his name . . . the one you used to share a desk with . . . "

Paltsiuk led Peltse down alleys, crooked backstreets, past garbage dumps and garages, out to the grove where the barracks used to be.

"Maybe it's all right." Peltse hesitated before following Paltsiuk into the ruins. "He wouldn't kill me, would he?"

Paltsiuk's briefcase did not contain two bottles of wine, as Peltse had first assumed, but rather a bottle of vodka and a glass stolen from a soft drink machine. Paltsiuk also produced some sausage and a package of cream cheese.

"Where the hell did you get this sausage?" Peltse blurted out. It was called "tea sausage," but in reality it more closely resembled cow dung.

Paltsiuk missed this. He was pouring vodka and telling Peltse how today he nearly got into a fight with the guy from the meat department, that mug-face Oriental who replaced Alik, you know.

Peltse warned that he wasn't going to down the whole glass.

"You just breathe out and swig it down like water . . . Don't think about it . . . "

Peltse did exactly that. But the vodka, instead of going down, somehow surged into his nose and eyes and squeezed out two large tears.

"Grab the sausage," Paltsiuk suggested helpfully. He couldn't bear to watch Peltse's suffering.

Peltse shook his head vigorously and stuffed the whole package of cheese into his mouth.

"I can't see life without meat, myself." Paltsiuk bit off half the sausage along with its stiff gut casing.

At last Peltse stopped coughing, wiped his eyes, and loosened two collar buttons.

"Where were you running?" asked Paltsiuk, and swallowed his liquor as if it were a soft drink. "I figure to some broad's, huh?"

"No, no," answered Peltse, "actually I was . . . "

"Hook me up with her!"

"No, I was, uh . . . on the way to my aunt's."

"What aunt's?"

"Not my aunt really, but uh . . . my mother's cousin."

"I see," said Paltsiuk. He also had an aunt who, after her daughter's death, lived alone in a two-room flat.

"The secret of successful discourse," wrote Levitov in a separate chapter, "lies in your ability to listen. Allow your interlocutor to express himself, give him your undivided attention, nod your head, don't hesitate to show your sincere interest and smile."

Peltse was all ears. He listened to how Paltsiuk's aunt had already agreed to exchange apartments with him. She was perfectly happy to move into Paltsiuk's spacious room in a communal apartment with shared bathroom and kitchen rather than pay triple for the extra square meters of living space—all the more so in view of those latest idiotic decrees and resolutions that effectively limit promises and guarantee restrictions in an already-complicated situation, you know.

The second shot of vodka hit the spot even better than the first, and Paltsiuk became increasingly more animated. He stepped over the fecal mounds and began urinating against the dilapidated barrack wall, which was generously covered with explicit drawings and the names of their artists.

"All would have been hunky-dory," he continued, "if only some son of a bitch hadn't talked her into asking for a separate apartment, and this (you can take my word for it!), . . . this could be done only through a multiple exchange and through a multiple exchange only."

"No kidding!" Peltse clung to Dr. Levitov's instructions religiously.

"What the heck, I asked her, do you need a separate apartment for? Your communal neighbor, I told her, will die sooner or later, right? And the whole apartment will be yours. That's all fine and dandy, she says to me. It would be nice if things went that way. But what if (get this!), what if I die first?"

Peltse was about to nod his head, but Paltsiuk interrupted the watering procedure, grabbed his briefcase, and took off.

"What's up?" Peltse called out anxiously.

"Cops!" Paltsiuk threw over his shoulder as he jumped out the window.

Peltse rushed to follow him, diving into bushes, under barbed wire, across ravines and hidden clearings, where stray dogs hide out for the night, where patients from the nearby infirmary wander out in hospital gowns to meet with their amiable nurses.

He caught up with Paltsiuk only where the private housing subdivision ended and the road began to show traces of cracked asphalt. Paltsiuk was holding onto a lamppost and expertly cursing the driver of the last trolleybus, who had refused to wait for him.

"Take it easy," Peltse told him, "these things happen."

The intense physical workout had alleviated his stressed condition, not without a little help from Paltsiuk.

"I have a book," confessed Peltse.

"What about dough?" Paltsiuk cut short his disclosure.

"What for?"

"What do you mean, what for?"

"Aren't the bars closed? It's half past one."

"There is one joint," Paltsiuk said, and ran to flag down a random Lada. The Lada stopped, and while Paltsiuk was talking to the driver Peltse stealthily counted the money in his wallet: a three-ruble bill, a ten, and some change. He carefully put aside sixty kopecks, added a couple more, dropped the whole lot into his pocket, and tucked away the wallet.

"Here, let's have it," said Paltsiuk, running up to Peltse.

"Well," asked Peltse, "is he giving us a lift?"

"Yep." Paltsiuk swiftly shoved his hand into Peltse's pocket and fished out the wallet.

"It's empty," Peltse protested. "All I've got is some change. Do you have any cash?"

Paltsiuk scooped up the silver, threw the wallet into his breast pocket, and bounded away.

"Wait!" Peltse was scared now.

"We'll sort it out later!" Paltsiuk hopped into the Lada.

"What about me?" shouted Peltse, running toward the car.

"Drop by any time," Paltsiuk said through the window as the car drove off. "At least once a week."

"That's it," Peltse decided. "No more Mr. Nice Guy. From now on it's strictly by the book. Sauna. Meditation. Massage. And sign up at the district."

4. Spot Check

THE DOOR OPENED AND PELTSE HIMSELF STEPPED INTO THE room from the dark.

"Good e-e-evening," he lusciously moved his lips, savoring every syllable.

The terrified Salupnev and Kavkadze sprang to their feet.

Peltse smiled slyly, pleased to see that his ploy had worked. The long wait in the ticket line, the bumpy ride in a bus packed with noisy, smelly farmers, a several-kilometer walk during which he concealed his all-too-familiar face in a wide hood—it had all paid off. And now that darkness had fallen, he softly knocked on the door as though he were some unwanted canvasser, turned the handle, and aimed his stern, probing glance at the two young candidates. How exactly do they spend their leisure hours and how do they justify the confidence that he, Peltse, placed in them?

The more experienced Salupnev swiftly regained his composure and, in a burst of enthusiasm, began to recite how happy they were to have Comrade Peltse drop by. The younger Kavkadze, just back this spring from Ethiopia, first flung himself toward the table, then stopped and pretended to be looking for a chair.

"Have a seat, please."

Peltse carefully scrutinized the table, didn't notice anything out of the ordinary, cast a quick glance under the bed, into the nooks and crannies, concluded that all the empty bottles must be hidden in the drawers, but decided to let it go.

"Thank you, I'm quite comfortable where I am."

Salupnev apologized for the mess. Today was a hectic, record-breaking day—all the teams performed at an average level of 124 percent, then he and Kavkadze summoned the group leaders for a report here and not to the club, because there, at the club, the youth were rehearsing a concert for the locals.

"That's good," Peltse sniffed suspiciously. Some time ago he had caught these two by surprise at the liquor store as they were stocking up on vodka and had severely reprimanded them. They grounded their defense on pending natural disasters: thunderstorms, torrential downpours, hail, or the possibility, for instance, that they might come down with pneumonia the night before and yet have to rally the troops the next morning.

"Mind you, guys," Peltse had said then, "I'll be keeping an eye on you."

Now he inquired about the details of their sojourn here and, listening to Salupnev's account, felt his gastric juices begin to flow in anticipation of the imminent catch.

"Discipline is also under control, knock wood," Kavkadze butted in.

"Is that a fact? You're sure, now?" It was dawning on Peltse that unless he shoved their faces into some obvious flaw right now, no one would offer him a well-deserved meal and drink. He took his time pacing around their modest quarters. Today's newspapers were laid out all over the table, charts and graphs recording the progress of the teams hung on the walls, as did Comrade Peltse's official portrait.

"And where have you posted *The Healthy Satirist?*"

"By the bulletin board, in the Red Corner."

"We have keep up the pressure on the lazy ones," stressed Peltse. "With criticism and humor. Humor, as you well know," he elaborated, "is a most proficient healer. So you go ahead and draw some idle ass sun-tanning in the field, and then watch him work that very ass off to atone for his misdemeanor."

His nose picked up the subtle, barely noticeable scent of a greasy snack that had, most likely, graced the table only moments ago. He stepped right up to Salupnev.

"Am I right, huh?"

Salupnev had been handpicked for leadership from the youth movement, where he had drawn attention to himself as a steel-willed yet adaptable chieftain. Before that, rumor had it, he was an unruly troublemaker who was expelled from college and, head shaved, shipped out to serve as a border guard. Having reviewed his options, he made a quick U-turn onto the correct path, distinguished himself, and obtained the necessary recommendations. After the army he became a student again, promptly gained momentum, and in an amazingly short time propelled himself upward to secure all that he had once so thoughtlessly discarded.

"We strictly follow your instructions," Salupnev said. "Without wavering a step."

His voice trembled as if he were about to burst into tears, because when he spoke he breathed inward instead of out. That was the reason why Peltse, no matter how hard he tried, could smell no more than aftershave.

"I don't believe it," he thought. "The younger one couldn't possibly handle that stuff."

He made yet another sweep of the room and caught sight of a green bottle neck sticking out of the pocket of a bulky foreign-made handbag. But it turned out to be a bottle of shampoo.

Salupnev, who had turned red and swollen while delivering his report, now walked over to the night table to get a pen and, with enormous relief, let out a lungful of air.

"Looks like they've smeared themselves with cologne and are about to go partying rather sit home and figure out ways to increase damned labor productivity," Peltse guessed uneasily, and added that good leaders should stand up for the interests of the cadre. "Because it's an open secret that locals are always stealing anything they can lay their hands on. To quote one recent example, they were paid for a given amount of bedsheet sets, but how many did they really distribute, you tell me!"

"Oh, we're no rookies in that department," Salupnev cheered up. He personally once caught the cook's assistants red-handed when they made a hole in a lump of butter and put in a brick to compensate for the loss of weight.

"And we, when I served in Ethiopia," boasted Kavkadze, "we built a sauna out of eucalyptus . . . "

"And I, when I was your age," Peltse interrupted, "I had to spend a night in the taiga out in the open air, in the devilish cold, and the temperature fell to -40 degrees Celsius! We piled logs crosswise, started a fire, and slept nearby on the pine branches!"

The recruits stood at attention looking straight ahead, their eyes fixed on Peltse, and tried hard not to breathe. From time to time Salupnev turned his head and exhaled over his shoulder through the corner of his mouth, while the inexperienced Kavkadze began to resemble a tomato.

Peltse assumed that Kavkadze was blushing from shame for never having spent a night in the taiga. Instead, he had already managed to take a trip abroad thanks to his daddy's connections and was now gliding up the correct path like butter on Teflon.

At the memory of bitter Siberian frosts Peltse was overcome by a desire for warmth, a hearty meal, and a chance to tell the fellows a thing or two about life.

"Where do you bastards hide your vodka?" he asked good-naturedly.

Salupnev immediately confessed that they had used up the vodka to rub down their feet during a cold snap, and Kavkadze also remembered using it as a head cleaner.

"You wash yours with vodka?!" Peltse asked, startled, and heard in response that the sound quality of music for local dances improves with cleaning.

"That's one thing I don't suggest. Dances attract all kinds of scum, they pull up fence posts with rusty nails sticking out . . . Have you fellows ever seen a person stricken with tetanus?"

His gangly subordinates fell silent and, it seemed to him, exchanged mocking smiles.

"Maybe you drank it, huh?" There was no hope left in Peltse's voice; rather, it quivered with reproach and despair. "Despite the fact that I nominated you two and not Mumuyev and Havelchenko."

He paused to let Salupnev and Kavkadze express their heartfelt gratitude. The situation was getting out of control. According to plan, his protégés were supposed to produce vodka and hors d'oeuvres, he was supposed to voice right-eous indignation, allow them to soothe him a bit, and then say, "Okay, fellas, now we'll find out if young people still know how to drink." And having thus inspired universal admiration (there's still fire in the old veins!), he would settle into a soft comfortable bed for the night.

"I'll be going now," he announced unexpectedly, gazing sadly into the tense faces of the candidates. "I will."

"Oh, no, not at this late hour," he was told. "Stay overnight."

And yet there was irony in the intonation, a hint of mockery and a touch of something sleazy. Peltse looked sus-piciously at Kavkadze's full lips, at Salupnev's elusive eyes, and thought, "What if they're . . . uh, you know . . . ?" He backed away toward the door.

"I'll be going," he repeated. "Into the night, down the empty road, singing, listening to the birds, enjoying the beautiful starry sky. All the people are asleep, even the hard-working trucks stand unattended in their garages. But! For reasons unknown, in the ditches on both sides of road gray shapeless figures lie in ambush, bicycle spokes protruding from their greasy overalls. And these spokes, strange as it make seem, have well-sharpened edges . . . Why would you say that is?"

The candidates stood dumbstruck.

"But I'm not afraid," said Peltse. "Leadership is not for the squeamish. Besides, I have this!"

He took out a knife and showed it to Salupnev and Kavkadze.

"So far, as you see, it is not open. But I can do this! . . . " He opened the knife and flashed its long blade in front of their noses.

The two uttered no sound. Neither knew the appropriate response.

"Well?" He stepped up to the candidates, took the knife in his left hand, and stretched out his right to his chosen two.

Salupnev had a vast meaty palm, which at this instant felt like a soggy frog. Kavkadze's hand had the feel of a soft, well-made kid glove, the kind you can only get abroad.

5. Peltse Is Ejected from the Brothel

IT HAS LONG BEEN NOTED THAT ON ANY GIVEN EVENING, IF one dares venture into a coffee shop, canteen, or some kind of greasy spoon, one is bound to spot somewhere in a remote corner two seated warrant officers. They have loosened their collar buttons and leaned over the table, their heads nearly touching. They have similar haircuts, similar garrison uniforms, similar shirts worn both loose and tucked in, similar jackets, shoulder straps, trousers, brown shoes, trench coats, hats, boots, underwear for summer and winter, similar field (khaki) and parade (woolen) uniforms, similar work clothes—hooded jumpsuits, bomber jackets, helmets, and shoulder belts. The only difference between the two men is that the craftier one has downed his glass, but not entirely, and an inch of liquor remains at the bottom. An empty bottle rolls around under the table. In the briefcase of one of the servicemen there is a reserve bottle of fortified wine. The other knows where one can procure cheap brandy at any hour of the day or night.

There may be no coffee in this coffee shop, no bread or even water, but the warrant officers are sure to be there. They can be found in other places as well, because, after all, they are men of service and not some derelicts who guzzle cologne in garbage dumps.

When a microbiologist opened the door to his hotel room one evening (on that particular evening the hotel was accepting only foreigners in addition to the microbiology convention delegates), he was greeted by his roommates, two warrant officers. They were singing the song "Blue Shoulder Straps"[*] but had completely forgotten the lyrics and recalled only the refrain.

"Blue shoulder straps," they sang, "blu-hoo shoulder stra-haps."

The microbiologist put down his bag, politely declined a drink, and walked out. By the time he returned, an empty bottle was roaming under the table, the officers were polishing off a second one, and were about to head out to the establishment where one can procure bandy regardless of the hour or season.

They sang a cappella about blue shoulder straps and gestured to their newfound friend that they would love to treat him. The scientist refused once again, went out to ride the trolleybuses, and returned only after public transit had shut down for the night.

In the room he found two warrant officers who looked as though their foreheads had grown together, but in reality

[*] A reference to the blue shoulder straps on the KGB uniform.—TRANS.

they were only supporting each other so as not to slip off key. They were singing a song called "Blue Shoulder Straps," or, more precisely, its refrain.

"Blue shoulder straps," resounded in the room, "blu-hooo-o-ooh shou-ho-oo-lder strahafs . . . "

Their garrison uniforms (i.e., military shirts, both loose and tucked in, jackets, shoulder straps, trousers, brown shoes, trench coats, and winter underwear) either stood on all fours, twisted and contorted, or, having crawled away into a corner, lay fast asleep.

"And have you seen, by any chance," the microbiologist addressed the two, losing not only his patience but evidently his mind, "the oil painting where Peltse is ejected from the brothel?"

"No, we have not," replied the one with the inch of vodka remaining in his glass, "because Comrade Peltse has never and would never go there."

He sprang to his feet, straightened out his crumpled jacket, and whisked down the corridor to make an urgent call at the front desk. He was immediately followed by his colleague, who was equally anxious to file a report; the latter, however, lost his way and realized this only in the rest room, where he was stopped in his tracks by a high-pitched female yelp.

6. Always with the People

"HAVE SOME MORE, PLEASE," SAID THE HOSTESS, HOPING somehow to invigorate the conversation. "You can't get food like this in a restaurant, you know."

She was wearing a dress made of a soft iridescent fabric that shimmered in the light and beguiled.

"Oh," said the guests. They had arrived only recently, but they figured out right away that not just anybody could get on the list for a dress like that.

"Some for you?" The hostess's voice resembled a meow as she scooped up a full ladle of something or other. She couldn't seem to distinguish their faces and kept mixing up their names, even though at work, when they delegated her to entertain the foreign colleagues, she was given a full list.

"Very tasty." The guests glued their eyes to the dress and sniffed the edibles suspiciously. Finally, an abrupt vowel sound shot from the mouth of the fellow wearing glasses, and all began to clang their forks in unison. Their matte standard-issue suits absorbed the electric light uniformly; their round-toed shoes, on the contrary, glistened, and pins bearing Peltse's head glowed on their left lapels.

"This is weird," the husband of the hostess thought to himself. The pocket of his suede blazer sported the logo of a brand of imported cigarettes.

"So, you came by train, did you?" He crossed his left ankle over his right knee, threw himself against the back of the armchair, stretched for his wineglass—and thus managed to fill a quarter of the spacious living room. The space he occupied, from the carved wall unit to the stereo system studded with knobs and levers, could easily have accommodated ten guests, if you lined them up in two rows of five apiece.

"By train," said the leader.

"By train," the others joined in. The selection of candidates for this trip was very strict, and they had all shown themselves worthier than worthy on all counts.

"And how do they prepare meat back home?" asked the hostess.

"Yes ma'am," answered the guests, not entirely understanding the question. The road had been a long one. In accordance with the instructions and in order to protect themselves from provocation, two slept while the third locked the compartment and stood guard for three hours, then woke up one of the other two and went to sleep in his place. It was like this both night and day. They cursed the hour they were selected for this trip and the colorful, subversive landscapes that kept leaping at the windows.

"So you must have gone through such and such countries and so and so cities?" asked the host. He didn't know how else to entertain these foreigners, who wouldn't drink and seemed to take such fright at the latest musical hits.

"We passed by them," answered the one who was shorter and broader than the others.

"And have you ever been there?" the others asked with respect.

"Just wondering," the host replied indifferently. He knew a lot, read widely, was able to do much; he was lucky, he was supported, even respected, although not yet feared.

"Aah!" The guests leaned back in their chairs and stretched out, but then suddenly they tensed up again, alarmed: Who is this person who knows so much, and why is he asking all these questions?

"Perhaps," suggested the lankiest of the three, who with his tiny clean face and clerk's hands could be mistaken for a schoolboy, "your work allows you to take an interest in life abroad?"

The guests stared into their plates and awaited an answer.

"Martians!" mumbled a friend of the host. He regretted coming, although there certainly was enough to drink.

"I wouldn't say so," the hostess's husband replied.

"Perhaps you'll have a drink after all?" insisted his friend. He had brought along a bottle of liquor, hoping to exchange it for something exotic.

"That middle one isn't bad," mused the dark-haired girlfriend of the hostess. "Look at those dark eyes flashing. Well, well, fearless leader. You're not much of a puritan, I'm afraid . . . "

"No, thank you," they refused unanimously.

"So, do you have families?" inquired the dark-haired friend.

"Yes."

Each one of them was a family man without a hint of reproach and had left at home as hostage a faithful wife and children with straight A's. As an extra precaution, the wife of the youngest conceived and gave birth to twins on the eve of his departure.

"And you must have children?" the hostess asked out of politeness. "They probably miss you . . . "

"Yes." The guests produced photographs from their wallets.

In two years of working abroad they were given a two-week holiday, which they were obliged to spend working in the basement of the embassy. They were not allowed to go home, but were allowed to receive one letter a month. The absence of a letter was a danger signal.

"And do you go abroad often?"

"Whenever it is necessary."

"I see . . . "

The guests were pleased with their answers and finished everything on their plates with a clear conscience. One of them whispered a question to his comrade in the glasses; the comrade thought about it for a minute and nodded his head. The third put his fork aside and also said something. The leader considered it and answered again with that same deep-throated sound. Two guests got up and headed in the direction of the bathroom. The hostess followed to show them where to turn on the lights.

Left alone without his compatriots, the leader looked at the cheerful brunette more boldly.

"Oh ho," she thought, and asked, "Shall we drink? It's considered very rude here to refuse a lady. You can get into big, big trouble!" She wagged her finger.

The guest grinned a toothy grin, although he had never studied this particular custom.

"So I'll pour you a glass?" She filled the goblets and said, "*Cin-cin?*"

He hesitated, but took the glass.

"Well then, down the hatch!" the dark-haired beauty commanded.

Hearing the water flush in the toilet, the seduced leader gulped down his glass, bugged out his eyes, went into a coughing fit, understood that this was all a trap, jumped up, wanted to hide on the balcony, hit himself against the chair, with the jovial lady shoving a mug of beer into his hand all the while.

His colleagues entered the room.

"You have so many books," they said.

"This is only a third of them." The host waved his hand. "The rest are in those rooms."

"And do you happen to have the works of Comrade Peltse?"

"Unfortunately . . . "

The guests exchanged glances. The leader cleared his throat, gave a signal to the lanky one, and they both walked out. The third one looked through the bookshelves, asked for permission, and pulled out a fat, colorful catalogue. He quickly leafed through the pages, paused at the one that displayed women in transparent undergarments, and propped the open book against his chest.

"Do you like it?" the rosy-lipped friend of the host inquired.

The leader and his lanky comrade appeared in the doorway carrying packages.

"No!" yelped the one looking at the pictures and covered the book with a napkin. "In our country we're not interested in such things!"

"Allow us," the leader announced, "to present you with a gift of the collected works of Comrade Peltse." And he handed out multi-volume sets in leather-bound boxes to the hostess, her husband, and to each of their friends.

"Oh!" said the hostess for all of them. "Did he write all this by himself?"

"No," she was told, "this is the gift edition. It contains

only Comrade Peltse's most renowned ideas. Unfortunately, neither his notes nor his answers to questions nor his bills and receipts are represented here."

"You don't say!" The hosts noticed that Peltse was slightly different on each of the pins, despite the fact that the red banner fluttered and the gold halo gleamed on all of them. The differences were hidden in the face, which at the hands of a skillful yet treacherous craftsman acquired distinctive human features. Sideburns lengthened by a micron turned Peltse into a philanderer, a line "accidentally" left on the face resembled a bruise, and a slightly pared-down jawbone revealed the signs of Down's syndrome.

The hosts and their friends lit up cigarettes. They were thinking that life everywhere takes its own course, and you never know when you'll run into a well-developed sense of humor.

"Are these the same as you have there?" asked the one who had been looking through the catalogue. He was pointing first at the cigarettes, then at the logo stitched onto the host's pocket.

"Yes," he was told, "help yourself."

"No," he jumped back, "I don't smoke."

"We don't smoke," repeated his colleagues.

"Does Peltse smoke?" asked the dark-haired lady and removed a fleck of tobacco from the tip of her tongue.

"No," answered the leader in a firm voice, "perhaps only during official receptions."

"When he is meeting with friendly delegations," added the others.

"And have you ever seen Peltse yourselves?" the hostess yawned loudly.

"Ourselves, no"—the leader had gone through special training sessions after work and knew the answers to all the questions—"but he is always with the people."

"Yes," piped up his friends, "he is always with the people."

7. Padding

IN THE EVENING, AS THE DOCTORS HAD ADVISED, PELTSE walked out to the riverbank to catch a breath of fresh air. Somewhere a train chugged by. In the old days leaves would drop off the trees from the clangor, but after Peltse ordered that rubber padding be installed under ten kilometers of track, the residents of the Great Leader's summer home promptly forgot that somewhere nearby sweaty passengers bump and lurch on the sardine express while the ever-irate conductors lie to them that the ventilators aren't working.

"Much has been achieved," Peltse thought to himself, and before his eyes gibbous human forms carved in granite stepped off the pages of schoolbooks rewritten on his ascent to power. Some wielded hammers, others proudly carried sickles. Behind them his chief cook, so weak and meek—for those were the years of national famine and heroism—crawled into his office with fish that merchant sailors and starving children had forwarded to the young Peltse. The cook held out the package, whispering, "The children . . . for you, Comrade sir . . . ," and, foaming at the mouth, he keeled over and died of starvation.

Peltse, moved greatly, saw to it that the "grocery stores" were renamed "groceterias," and, having considered the options for "dry goods," decided to leave them as they were. And, by the way, there are few who know that is was precisely he who came up with the idea of a national all-out war on harelip in medicine.

He still remembers how some had said to him: Maybe we should beat a retreat, turn around, shift into reverse, make a reactionary U-turn, advance to the rear, recoil into the dark past. To the place where it's damp and where the smell of rotting cheese hangs in the air. They offered him sausage and silver, the power and the glory, the dust and the fury, satin and sushi, megabytes and shining lights, sugar-free gum and idiot-proof cookies . . . They were willing to flood us with soap and Pepsi, just to prevent the merger of our cable car networks.

Peltse remembered those days and began to snort.

"Pay them no mind!" wailed the throngs of children to whom he had granted the joy of childhood and permission to dance the tango. Millions of youngsters had come out then for the fitness pageant, and Peltse was not able to hide his beneficent grandfatherly smile, which so frightens those who get in our way.

And now, having drunk of the salubrious air, as the doctors advised, he stood as if in a painting, a field of rye rising over the knee yet below the belt, and up above he saw that each cloud hosted a choir of boys about to sing the greenfinch song, while the girls, dressed up as little froggies, cast up envious glances from down below.

"Their turn will come later," thinks Peltse, "even though they do develop faster."

"Not everyone all at once," Peltse says to them and squats down. "Each in his own time."

"One was run over by a truck," he remembers the facts of history, "another died of a stomach infection as he was having a tooth pulled, a third stepped on a shovel and got it in the head . . . And all were comrades, knights of unanimity, victorious giants . . . "

A bit of mist clouds his eye, he swallows a large gulp of fresh air, and thinks that people like that are not to be found anymore . . .

"There is one, though, isn't there . . . A new boy, what's his . . . Shabangabuck, I think. He never says anything, and yet I've got this funny feeling . . . Hmm . . . Such a strange little fellow . . . Shabangabuck . . . Can't imagine what kind of fate he'll have . . . Although," Peltse yawns and partakes of the transparent evening air one more time, "he'll take whatever we have in store for him, won't he?"

Darkness fell. The boys' choir droned on with the cricket song. The basses from the girls' chorus joined in accompaniment. Peltse's lips grew moist. He suddenly imagined tiny toddlers on skates pattering toward him from all directions. And each of the chubbies in the most adorable sports outfit! They rush up and start pressing their little bodies against Grandpa Peltse. And here come the girls, slithering out of their teeny lily pond. A boy on one side, a girl on the other. Now, now, shame on you! You'll poop your dear grandpa out completely if you keep this up.

Peltse unbuttoned his collar and was just about to take in a fresh dose of oxygen when he heard a long-forgotten sound. Somewhere, quite close, train tracks convulsed, beating against the grease-covered crossties.

"The padding gave out," Peltse guessed, "or else some bastard pinched it. And the alarm system didn't work!"

"Much has been achieved," he thought, listening to the melody being furiously clashed out by the train wheels, "but there is still much to be done."

"Sha-ban-ga-buckshabanga-buckshabanga-buck" was what Peltse and all those who at that time were in his closely guarded dacha heard.

8. In the Third-Class Sleeper

"SO WHAT DO YOU THINK?" ASKED THE YOUNG MAN WHO HAD immediately introduced himself as a student of the military college. The lights were already out, but listening to his voice you could guess his facial expression—sincere, naive, a little dopey.

After a long pause, the man on the upper ledge across from the cadet cautiously remarked that this question was not one of the simpler ones, and that it was proper to wait and see how the official circles, those more familiar with the issues, would respond.

"I heard," a woman from the lower berth spoke up, "that he didn't really die."

"What do you mean he didn't die? We had a special lecturer come by who said his death was the result of mushroom poisoning."

The man from the upper ledge cleared his throat and ventured, "It wasn't mushrooms, it was mushroom soup from a can."

The woman laughed.

"Really, Peltse croaking from canned soup! All they eat is caviar and champagne. My daughter's in-laws—and on Firemen's Day it will be exactly ten years since my darling Irochka got married (it's so hard to believe!)—more precisely him, Talik's father, used to study with Fakov himself . . . "

"I'm saying this"—the man on the upper ledge, a veterinarian of about sixty, was offended—"because I know! He went to the village where he was born. The food situation there is hopeless, of course . . . Nothing but soap and vinegar. He made himself some soup from a can, the intestines twisted over, volvulus, spasms, kaput!"

"God forbid!" the woman's voice skipped down to a stage whisper. "I'll tell you, no matter how well you set yourself up in life, no matter what kind of clout you end up having (when you're young, you know, it's this and it's that, you have to have your fun—aah, don't you think so?), later you're always drawn back to the place you were born. It's like in that song that Maryna, what's her name, you know, on TV, the one she first did New Year's Eve . . . "

"How will things be now, I wonder?" mused the cadet dreamily.

Everyone fell silent. Someone came down the corridor and stumbled.

"Peltse was so . . . Well, how can I put it . . . " In a few quick movements the woman turned over to face the wall, adroitly tucked the blanket under herself, and sighed, "He loved life so much!"

It was obviously years and years before she would have to contemplate the onset of old age.

"Lecher!" the veterinarian blurted out. "In the positive sense of the word, of course."

"Is it true that they (those that want to, of course), that they can all have their old organs transplanted?" The young student was trembling, because he wanted to know the truth.

"Sure is!" answered his neighbor. "Who would refuse new organs? You yell your head off at work every day, the old gland goes out of whack, and no matter how hard you whip it, the bitch just won't function like it used to. When you're forty, it's still not too bad, but after that you don't even bother anymore."

"What do you mean . . . ?" The cadet wasn't following.

"You're absolutely right," the woman yawned, "especially the military men. Very stressful work. But you can run into exceptions there, too, let me tell you . . . "

"In my opinion," the cadet defended his own, "everything depends on the particular person. If you work out regularly, get involved in sports, move around a lot . . . They're very clear about this in our courses and, besides, I read myself that one doctor in the Philippines did research on baboons, and he says that every day a human being must . . . "

"Baboons!" the vet interrupted. "A baboon doesn't have a care in the world! Sits down under a pineapple, picks itself a banana . . . "

"And when are they supposed to get involved in sports?" The woman flipped over to her right side again. "Every minute there has to be accounted for. And when you're on vacation, you're either entertaining someone or . . . not to mention meeting delegations at the airport . . . And you say 'lecher'! On the contrary, Peltse was very interested in art. Our in-laws, Zoya, to be precise, and she's the type that doesn't miss a thing . . . "

"I said no such thing, ever, to anyone," the vet raised his voice. "I merely wanted to note that at a given moment, under certain circumstances, various factors can influence the course of events. You know yourselves what great attention is paid to productive criticism these days. And I feel that this is very proper and correct. We must, finally, bring in some law and order. Shabangabuck stated this plainly . . . I presume you do read the papers?"

"The third question on our finals is always on Shabangabuck's speech or on a document from his papers," admitted the cadet.

"Well, you can say what you want, but I know that Shabangabuck and Peltse were like this," the woman made a sign to her interlocutors, "like hand and glove. Both loved to fish. Day after day at the fishing pole, while the home, the children, school, looking after the house was, of course, left up to us women. Not to mention that each of them had a couple of nannies, however many he felt he needed. But we're not complaining, it's a woman's fate, after all." She was quiet, but not for long. "Well, I think it's wonderful that Shabangabuck is Number One now. Because suppose they chose one of the young ones—he's going to want some of this and then he'll get a craving for some of that. There'll be no stopping him! But this one here's already got everything, and Peltse knew him well, and don't you forget that Peltse was handpicked and blessed by Kapsho himself!"

"Yes"—the cadet had long been waiting to say something very appropriate—"Peltse was a man made from Kapsho dough and leavened with Kapsho yeast, even though he did criticize him. Here, I'm inclined to think, he overdid it a little. He should have said that well, yes, there were some shortcomings, but not undermine everybody's faith like that, especially the youth. Just take a look at what's going on with the civilians. They do say, however, that the exhibition at the Central Museum has been augmented by some artifacts of the Kapsho era, but I still haven't made my way over there, I'm embarrassed to say."

"Yep," the veterinarian said, "Kapsho, he was a tough guy."

"But what else could he do?! There were enemies every-where," the cadet explained. "I read, I have this book at home, and it's got everything in there, all the trials. Even the case of the chimney sweeps, all the deviations, the protocols of the so-called Society of Sincere Gratitude . . . It's just that they were very skillful at disguising themselves back then."

"There were a hell of a lot of spies, too," the woman spoke up. "Though there are just as many now, they've all gone undercover."

"Yeah . . . He sure caught a lot of them." The veterinarian's head dangled from the bunk above. "Swedish, Norwegian, from some kind of Manhola or Mancutta, remember the one stealing fire extinguishers? But he never did catch the main guy, Cumbush. And why was that? How come, I ask you, huh?"

No one spoke up.

"Because that snake, that scumbag, he pretended he was his friend, so he took him in, gave him a good job, money, an apartment, a medal, absolutely everything, and then he goes and turns out to be a spy."

"Who?"

"Cumbush! It was because of him, they say, that all those injustices occurred, because they were sending him instructions from abroad, and then he'd go to him . . . "

"Who?"

"Kapsho, who else?! Yes sir! So then, such and such is happening, he'd say, give me the security pass. And he, of course, couldn't even imagine such foulness—take it, he'd tell him, just watch what you do with it . . . So then he—whoosh, scoops up the pass and takes off. He used to ride around town in a cab, and if a girl caught his eye, he'd just have to point his finger in her direction . . . It was bad stuff . . . "

"Excuse me," the cadet asked respectfully, "did you by any chance take part in the liberation of Constantinople?"

"No," said the veterinarian, "but I do collect books about

war, and I have one very rare edition about all those prime ministers. It was," his voice dropped down to a whisper, "taken off the library shelves!"

"And I heard," the woman related, also whispering, "that Peltse wasn't really dead."

"How could he not be dead? What about the funeral? What about the body?"

"A double! Don't you understand? They must have come up to him and said, you've gotta go, you know. What would you do in his place?"

"Well, for a million I might consider it," the cadet said thoughtfully.

"I think it's a dummy," the vet threw in. "They're a lot easier to embalm, 'cause by the time you throw the guts out . . ."

"Oh, stop, stop, please," pleaded the woman, "or I'll be sick in a minute."

"You can afford to be sick, but the medics are used to everything, that's what they get paid for."

"If you took me to a morgue, I would just die in there!"

"We were playing soccer once," reminisced the student, "and my head was smashed open with a rock . . ."

"So where did he go then," the vet interrupted, "Peltse, that is, if he didn't die?"

"I don't know," said the woman, "into the taiga, I guess . . ."

"They say he'd been begging to leave for a long time, but they wouldn't let him. Besides . . ."

"I don't blame him!" The vet once again prevented the cadet from divulging the contents of a highly classified lecture at the academy. "What does he need it for? No matter which way you turn, everything's a bloody mess. All over the country. I wanted to travel second class, came to get my ticket ten days ahead of time—we don't have any, she says. The two-bit snotnose! You're still wet behind the ears, missy, I tell her. You could be my, you know . . . I mean, I could be your . . ."

Someone desperately knocked on the wall and an outraged elderly voice whined, "Cut it out! 'Boo-boo-boo, boo-boo-boo.' The day isn't long enough for you people, or something?"

The conversation stopped short. A moment later a passenger with a heavy suitcase knocked his head against the cadet's feet and swore. In the meantime, the suitcase painfully crushed the feet of the fourth passenger in the compartment, who was lying in the lower berth across from the woman. During the entire trip he hadn't uttered a word and kept covering his face with a newspaper.

"I've sure raised a fine lot," moaned Peltse, grasping his injured foot as he hid under the blanket. But by now his neck was so red and irritated by the fake beard that sleep was out of the question.

9. The Loss of Peltse

ONCE UPON A TIME A MAN WENT DOWN TO THE WARM seaside. Time went by, but the weather there just wouldn't let up—wind, waves, cold, and rain day after day. After a while he spent all he had, and as the time to leave approached, he decided to treat himself to the best dry wine as a memento of this sunny land.

"Today I'll hit the hard stuff for the last time (vodka would be best), but starting tomorrow I'll drink only dry wine." He would deceive himself this way almost every day. Or, to be more precise, "every" day as long as the money lasted.

And so on the eve of his departure, already quite late in the day, he made his way toward the wine cellar, where all kinds of vintages lay idle in wooden casks in the cold and dark. He was met at the door by a bearded storekeeper, an enormous fellow, dark and stern. His large sinewy arms looked as though they had spent a lifetime mixing clay from dawn until dusk.

The man asked for something to drink and the storekeeper drew some wine from the nearest cask.

"Is this good wine?"

"You won't complain."

"How much?"

"I'm not charging you."

The man took the wine cup, tipped it, and drank the whole thing. The wine was indeed dry, sour actually. Perhaps I should try another kind, he thought, let the two mix together, the effect might be stronger.

"I'd like some from this one." He tapped his finger against the fattest barrel.

And so that man drank and drank, as the storekeeper served him one dry vintage after another—white, red, amber, and the nobly dark.

"Well?" the host finally asked.

"Very good." The man pretended to be drunk, but the storekeeper saw right through him.

"Perhaps you've got something hidden," pleaded the man, "in your deepest chamber, something very very rare, just for your own, you know, the kind where one gulp makes your feet spin and your head crystal clear?"

"All right," said the hairy winemaker, "I'll bring you my best wine, pressed years ago by my great-great-great-grand-father."

And he walked out.

The man tried the ancient liquid—it simply had no effect. The storekeeper didn't take offense, didn't curse him, didn't throw him out. He turned his back and disappeared among the vats, casks, and clay pots, returning with the most unique of wines. The man began to slurp it—it had no taste.

"Do you like it?" the storekeeper asked.

"I'm in heaven," the man lied sincerely. "This is it! My head's as light as a feather and my feet . . . "

"And what does it remind you of?"

The man fell to his knees and confessed that it didn't remind him of anything.

"Go away," said the storekeeper.

"Save me," the man begged, "and take pity on me. My vacation is over and my money is gone."

"So what the hell do you want from me?"

"I need it, very very much . . . ," the man crawled up closer, "rather, I can't go on at all without it."

"What am I to do with you, huh?" sighed the vintner-and-potter-in-one.

"Have mercy!"

"Well, all right, come with me."

Without further ado, the bearded man led Peltse down the sturdy steps, through the wooden door, into the depths of his cellar.

And we never saw him again.

10. The Minstrel

COME ON UP A LITTER CLOSER, MILORDS AND MILADIES, I got something to si-hi-hing fer you. For whosoever wants to know of the tale of Peltse warms the cockles of my aged heart. Just tell me who sent you here and where you're from, my little clever ones, as I do not possess, unfortunately, the faculty to behold you, my darling doves, for sightless am I, but if you write your names down in this book right here, it'll be my keepsake for ever and eve-he-he-her.

And which song shall I sing for you? Because I got one to suit every taste. I got one about his humility, how he would ride to work every day on a rickety old streetcar, how he shut down the special trough shops for our top snouts, how he would slam a nail into fancy furniture when he couldn't find a place to hang his weathered coat. I got a heroic one, too . . . Hey, what's that clinking in your bags there? Don't be shy now, my glass is right here, let's have it . . . more . . . more . . . yo! Sufficient . . . Well, God bless . . . Hmm . . . Purr-r-dy good . . .

So ya wanna heroic one? 'Bout the white knight Peltse, and how for three days they slashed 'im, they pierced 'im, may his soul rest in pea-he-he-he-ce . . . It was on the Feast Day of Our Blessed Mother Mary the Protectress, may we all live to see it in the coming year . . . So you're interested in this kind of stuff, are you, my little spiritual fledglings? And which wise man taught you all this? Which one was it? The times are uncertain nowadays, for we all walk in the shadow of Shabangabuck, may his name be anathema, but then we're not talking about him, are we, but about Peltse, who could be neither drowned by water nor burned by fire . . .

Hey you, how about another swig, my voice is starting to give out. Thanks. Well, here's to all of you. It's so great that our youth still has an appreciation for the past, 'cause that's where you'll find all of our glo-ho-ho-ry. So who sent you over to see me, my children, if it's not too big a secret? Have you all signed the book yet? No? Yeah, yeah, I'll play for you, of course I will! You want a sad one? About how they threw Peltse down on the cold bare earth in the jailhouse, in the sla-ha-ha-ha-mer? So then . . . Oh, they threw him down on that there cold bare earth in the slammer, and he lay there, poor wretch, on the filthy, the spittled, the slobbered . . .

Hey, what about me? Yeah, so what? So cheap already at your tender age, shame on you! For your information, my dear young friend, all my texts get a lot better after a little medicinal treatment of the vocal cords. That's more like it! Well, may each of you live with whoever you want! Who-ooh! Good stuff! Firewater . . .

What happened next? When? Ah, oh yeah! So, our noble and gallant Peltse's lying there, oh he sure is, on the spittled cold bare earth, sobbing and listening ever so attentively if someone's coming to the rescue. You're a fool, real fool,

Harkun says to him, silent as stone on the upper bunk. And this Harkun was once upon a time his chief rival, until Peltse persuaded Kapsho to transfer him into the dungeons. Why don't you, says Harkun now to Peltse, take out the basin with excrements? Take it out, take it out, urge the big ugly bandits and murderers, for if you don't we shall slit your throat. Is that any way to behave, I ask you all, is it? Can't hear you. What do you mean "why"? I can't hear you, 'cause I'm hard of hearing. I'll have a little more right in here . . . No more?! You sure? You wouldn't, by any chance, make me sing and then leave me while you're, you know . . . Well, watch yourselves . . . What? The one about Peltse's prophecy? Okay, I'll believe you. But this is gonna be the last time, so listen up.

Hey, hey, there will come such a time, such a day, hey!
When Shabangabuck will be no more, damn them all!
And an emperor dumb, behind glass, with no clothes on,
     will sit in his place, yes!
This will be in the year so far hence, who knows whence?
Then one day he'll set out on his annual inspection and
     travel afar.
He will stumble on Peltse, all filthy and hairy and dagger-
     nailed crouched in a hole.
And he'll jump back in horror and fall like a crux to the
     ground and repent!
May the Good Lord have mercy on us!

. . . What's all that giggling? Don't you believe he'll repent? I don't believe it either. "Crux"? How am I supposed to know? It's written down "crux," I sing "crux." This is folk stuff, you know, not some stand-up comic act or pop song. Peltse in the sex shop? You must be kidding. No, never heard of that one. I repeat, this is not rock, this is . . . Who are you guys, anyway? Aaah! . . . Why didn't you say so in the first place . . . Very glad, very glad to meet you . . .

Which department? Actually, I'm on the payroll with the folk department, but the damn bookkeepers . . . No reports filed for two months? Let me explain! I did not submit last month's report, because . . . No, no! I mean, yeah! I filed one this month, on the twentieth, and it covered two months . . . Aah, don't be so hard on me . . . Besides, for such honored guests I've always got . . . Right there, behind the icon. I'll never do it again, I promise. Yes, yes, pull it out and help yourselves! What's the toast?

Why wasn't I singing on the boulevard? It was raining like hell and, besides, I still didn't get my overtime bonus for last month. But mainly it's because of my new guide (I got a new one again, you know), he's the one that didn't . . . No! Never mind what he says! Let him show you the medical certificate, although he's the kind of jerk that can bribe his way around anybody! Not like me, I always stick to the rules! I went out for the memorial days, I did so, and out to the monument, too. And now you tell me, where the hell are my two legitimate days off, why don't you tell me that, huh? Just like we agreed! Because revolutionary zeal is all fine and dandy, but I'm sick and tired of struggling for justice all the time, in vain, I might add. My goddamned vocal cords are torn to bloody pieces! Pour me another, my friend. Thanks. Well, here's to rock and roll! . . . Who-ooh! This is no joke! Steeped with wort, Saint-John's-wo-o-o-ort! Yeah!

Hey, what if this is all a dream? And it's so hard to breathe because my nose is stuck in the pillow? What if I make the effort, turn over, shout out at the top of my lungs, and then I'll wake up? Young and alive, on my own two feet, free, my eyesight back . . .

PENTAMERON

or

*A Glimpse into the Lives of Five Employees
at a Scientific Research Institute*

NAME OF INSTITUTION: NIIAA

NAMES OF EMPLOYEES:

Ophelia Feliksivna Lemberg, head of the Editorial
    Section of the Department of Scientific and Technical
    Information
Antonina Pavlivna Smyrnova, senior editor
Svitlana Zhuravlynchenko, editor
Zoyka Vereshchak, translator in the Foreign Contacts
    Group of the Department of Scientific and Technical
    Information
Vitya Maliatko, translator in the above-mentioned group

LOCATION: Room 507, on the fifth floor of the new building

The action takes place in one of the years of a bygone era.

■ □ ■ □ ■

Ophelia Feliksivna Steps into the Room First

BUT THE DRAFTSWOMAN, WHO LIVES SOMEWHERE WAY OUT where the dogs bark, is already rolling down the hall from the toilet toward her. The draftswoman cooks up a pot of spuds and cracklings for her family at dawn, strides through the mud to the commuter train, and an hour and a half or two later she can be found, in the best of moods, removing her galoshes in the lobby.

"Howdy, Feelia Feelixivna. And why are you so late? Ten to, and still not at your post? If you got up earlier, you'd have less of those aches and pains."

The draftswoman holds the engineering position, stands four feet nine inches tall, and is afraid of nothing.

"You guttersnipe!" Ophelia Feliksivna would like to reply, unmoved, her dignified voice cold with disdain, but a jittery, awkward, and completely unwelcome "G-g-good morning" leaps out instead. Repressed anger scalds her nerves, the key rattles in the keyhole, the door won't open.

However, she says to herself, "I am calm, I have the power and the wisdom to control my feelings," and her indignation subsides a little. "And now," Ophelia Feliksivna instructs herself as she turns away from the draftswoman's broad backside, "I shall focus on the positive."

She tears off yesterday's page from the calendar and learns that today the balance between night and day is to shift in favor of daylight, and this encourages her. Another happy fact is that last night she took no pills at all and slept eight hours. Ella got her these imported pills from the pharmaceutical stock of the Central Committee before she left. It's a year and a half already since they've been OUT THERE. They left everything behind—job, car, apartment, summer home, Yura's party membership card, the curses of their parents. All for the sake of Karina. What future did she have here? Yesterday Genia got a letter that made it clear Yura is still driving a cab, Ella has started doing manicures, and they have enough to live on. Karina goes to school, gets an A every day, and works in a store three days a week. In half a year she'll be sixteen. It's time to start thinking about a second car. You can forget about the pills, they write. Pills out here cost as much as a fur coat. And the rest of the money goes for insurance. It's best that you keep corresponding through Genia; they wouldn't take her pension away, after all. And in the meantime, get in touch with Kama (she works for Intourist) and try to find some reliable American, get to know him, and pass along those hair curlers Ella sewed into that pillow that wouldn't fit into the suitcase, you know, the one with the extra weight that was turned back by customs. How can you live there in the midst of such utter vulgarity!

I must water the flowers, Ophelia Feliksivna tells herself. And open the windows right away. She takes the carafe and walks down to the end of the corridor.

The elevator doors open and people burst out onto the fifth floor. They are: the girls (typists), the personnel of ERA Duplicating practically in full complement, and Antonina Pavlivna Smyrnova, editor from 507.

Last Night She Had a Dream

SHE SAW HER NINE-YEAR-OLD SON GROW WEAKER AND WEAKER before her eyes, she heard the mucus gurgle in his chest, felt his jabbing and cutting stomach pains.

For some reason all this is happening in a trolleybus. The passengers are shouting: It's that new strain of flu! Dysentery! Sunspot activity! A war veteran has blocked the aisle, demands attention, wants to tell everybody how murderous paramedics once tried to yank out his appendicitis with no anesthetic. A glass of 100-proof down the hatch and forward march!

Andriy squeals and kicks his feet like a teething infant. Antonina Pavlivna grabs the child and runs out, slippers on bare feet, to see the district doctor.

"Well," the pediatrician says to her, "you've really done it! Now you'll find out what it means to avoid booster shots! Not to turn in timely blood-urine-stool samples! Not to broaden your child's horizons with all the latest methodologies! Not to build up his immunity while still in the womb! Not to take him for tennis and English lessons! Oh no, no, only surgical intervention can save him! All you were worried about was free health care! Rather than think of the incorruptible and eternal! Where is my rusty scalpel?!"

"Have mercy!" Antonina Pavlivna cries, sobs, and whimpers somewhere far away, tearing at the cobwebs around her until she finally breaks out of the nightmare and into the present day.

"What will happen, I wonder?" she whispers when back in her bed once more.

"What's that?" Volodya, her husband, jumps at her from his own nightmare.

They both tiptoe up to their son. Andriyko has curled into a little ball, his legs stick out like two icicles, his forehead is burning, and the blanket is on the floor.

From seven-thirty on, Volodya is at the phone trying to

get a doctor. But evidently some lazy broad is manning the lines at the clinic today. She probably lifted the receiver and forgot to put it back, or stuck it diagonally somehow, and has now planted her ass on the already-broken unit and is yapping away with the girlies on the usual dumb women's topics. Volodya is becoming more and more irritated; in a few minutes he will demolish the phone. But how can you not see his point! They agree that he will stay home with Andriy in the morning, and that she will beg off work from Ophelia in the afternoon. Volodya also works in a research institute, but they get bonuses and they get to go to Moscow-Leningrad pretty often, because their institute is in the special category that has a post office box for an address.

"Run over to the clinic! You can be late for work!" Volodya demands. "The house calls list closes at eight! You know they're crooks!"

In the bedroom Andriy sits up, coughs, and calls for his mother.

"Wait!" Volodya says to him.

Only after she has opened the door, Antonina Pavlivna notices the dust clinging to the telephone stand like hoarfrost, the scissors that Volodya used last night to cut out the TV listings, and the scent of rot and decay coming from the kitchen garbage pail.

"What is it now?" Volodya is pushing her out the door.

"Cabbage," Tonya explains. "Give me the pail, I'll throw it out quickly. You'll choke to death in here!"

"Run!"

"I'm begging you," she pleads. "Why can't you understand! Fresh air—bronchi, the lungs! . . . "

"Goddamn . . . their mothers!" Volodya shoves her out. "And at one-thirty you'd better be here!"

"And put away those scissors!" she calls from the exit toward the door that has just slammed shut, padded with depressing black vinyl and stitched in a large diamond design. "Because if, God forbid, Andriy should step . . . "

She is lucky enough to catch a ride, at the clinic she arranges for a doctor's visit with no problem, the trolley gets her to the square in no time, and there a moonlighting shuttle bus makes an unexpected appearance, thanks to which Antonina Pavlivna whisks through the entrance on time, and today her name will not be entered on the blacklist. The elevator lifts her to the fifth floor, bangs against the top beam, and rumbles down for more cargo.

"Pheww!" Antonina Pavlivna can't believe her luck. "I'm not late after all!"

The Radio Says It's Nine O'Clock

OPHELIA FELIKSIVNA WATERS THE FLOWERS. SVITLANA Zhuravlynchenko is putting on makeup at her desk. Antonina Pavlivna walks out to wash her hands.

"Can you believe it, Antonina Pavlivna, downstairs they're writing down the names of everyone who's even one second late!"

That's Zoyka Vereshchak greeting her from the resonant depths of the dingy corridor. Now that she has tripped out of the elevator she's in no big hurry to get to the room; instead, she darts into the sanitary facility to remove her heavy woolen bloomers and slip into lighter cotton ones.

Another fifteen minutes go by and a breathless Vitya Maliatko bounds up the fifth-floor stairs. He has slept in, as usual, and is decidedly late, but he has outfoxed the guards. The boys from the basement machine shop were unloading some large metal-edged crates at the entrance. He grabbed the heaviest, backed in through the lobby, pretended to be tying his shoelace, and then one blink of an eye and he's gone. What's the problem?! He got here ahead of everybody. He doesn't have his number because he forgot to take it, and he forgot to take it because he got a sudden attack of stomach cramps. He just spent half an hour going through hell in the bathroom. Prove it isn't so!

"You ape," Ophelia Feliksivna says to him.

Vitya jumps over to hug her, spills a glass of water on some office barricades on the way, grasps the lady's hand, kisses it, and presses it to his heart.

"Hippopotamus!" Ophelia Feliksivna feigns indignation. "Look what you've done! Go get a rag and clean it up!"

Vitya repents, bows down low, and in one breath slurps up the puddle.

"Yuck!" Zoyka grabs her stomach. "I'm going to throw up!" And she shoves the bloomers into her bag.

Vitya Maliatko simulates nausea, groans, trembles, but all of a sudden ceases his antics, having noticed on the windowpane what is unquestionably a natural wonder, begotten of water and ice and worthy of depicting and preserving for all eternity. He rushes to his desk and rummages through the drawer for a pen.

Vitya Maliatko Works as a Translator

LIKE ZOYKA, HE IS A MEMBER OF THE FOREIGN CONTACTS Group, headed these days by Comrade Woodnov.

The sun does not wait for Vitya Maliatko to capture his composition on paper. It melts the crystalline sheet, and beauty dissipates before his eyes in tiny rivulets zigzagging down warped glass.

Vitya first squints his left eye, then his right. The blotch over the cactus reminds him of an ice hole in the river. And the roof of the building behind the auto depot looks like a human head. On wintry nights he whose head this is probably scratches his way up the austere walls of NIIAA, breaking his nails on the gutters, sinking his teeth into the bricks, and then by dawn, his strength gone, collapses against the windowpane. Where those tricklets are—that's the mouth. And there you've got white teeth, a nose flattened against the glass, unshaved cheeks. What a brilliant painting this could be! One twenty by eighty. Mixed media.

Vitya Maliatko wants to be a painter. He's twenty-six now, but all is not lost. Van Gogh was thirty when he began.

"Why don't you take your coat off?" Zoyka Vereshchak asks. "Don't tell me you've finished your translation already?"

"Umhuh."

"Show me."

"Come see. Just wash your hands first."

"You're lying. You haven't even looked at it."

Zoyka sits, trying her best to delay the joy of encounter with a German periodical that every month, for God only knows what reason, arrives at the NIIAA library. Her job is to translate the titles of all the articles, annotate them, and turn them in to the library. In addition, she conscientiously translates letters, invitations to conferences, chapters from— to her mind—completely incomprehensible technical books and instruction manuals. That is why she is chronically overworked, while Vitya has nailed the jargon down and regularly knocks off annotations to American journals guaranteed to keep even the curious from wanting to open them. "Here you bust your ass just to get some goddamn cement or brick," the engineers who read his translations complain to each other, "and those Americans are doing fucking ferro-concrete aerobics . . . "

Finally Vitya gets up, hangs his coat on the rack, and returns to his desk. Awaiting him is a mammoth volume of papers on quality control presented at an international conference in Tokyo at the juncture of March and April last year.

This book was brought in by the director himself, Yevhen Yevhenovych Mudrava. In June he was part of a delegation that visited the Netherlands, and there he met a participant in the Tokyo conference, Gelsemino Abdun-Nur, who can speak seventeen languages and who, as a token of friendship, gave Mudrava this volume, bound in imitation leather, within which Abdun-Nur's short article on the use of solar energy for heating swimming pools in the town of Pasadena, California, also makes something of a splash.

Mudrava's institute, NIIAA, does not directly concern itself with questions of quality. However, as a professional, scholar, and prudent administrator, Mudrava knows: Five, ten, twenty, or, let's say, even fifty years will pass, and we will come to realize that the neglect of quality is a crime, and then we will pull from the archives the Tokyo conference on quality (which never did get even a two-word mention in our press), and we will recognize, finally, those who in those distant (and not so simple!) times had their fingers on the pulse of progress.

Lupova, head of the Department of Scientific and Technical Information, solemnly presented Vitya Maliatko with Abdun-Nur's gift about a month ago and set the deadline: five days for translation from first word to last, to be executed with a sense of personal commitment, as is fitting when one deals with foreign capitalist publications paid for by the state in cold hard cash.

"Orally?" Vitya asks.

"In writing," Lupova commands. "This is a job from the director!"

"But there are four hundred pages here!"

"So what? Half of them aren't even full. Look here, you've got one paragraph on top and the rest of the page is completely empty! They don't skimp on paper, they've got it all out there. Besides, I notice that they have a habit of repeating certain words several times. So you don't have to go into the dictionary for each one. Just make sure you write legibly. The typist is always complaining about you."

Vitya Maliatko is not upset, because he has a well-grounded suspicion that strung-out Lupova will forget all about quality in twenty minutes. So will the director, who from his entire trip to Holland (in one week they saw the Kunstkamera, and the museum with the black tulips, and a series of industrial projects) recalled most vividly a black man in the discount department store to which their entire delegation was delivered by bulging bus on the eve of their departure. The size of the black man was remarkable: he blocked the whole aisle. His head was overgrown with tiny braids with ribbons and beads. And while the director groped every price tag, trying to sniff out which of the T-shirts was cheapest, the black man carelessly floated down aisles of merchandise, pulling out with one long brown finger a shirt here or pair of pants there, and, not looking at it all that carefully, tossing it into his cart with disgust.

"So how much have you translated? Tell the truth!" Zoyka Vereshchak wants to know.

"Twenty . . . twenty-four pages," lies Vitya Maliatko.

"Wow!" says Zoyka, and quickly dives into her still-unvanquished but scrupulous text about the new thermoinsular properties of some polymer she's never heard of.

Ophelia Feliksivna Places Her Hand on the Receiver

SHE WANTS TO PHONE SOMEONE, BUT HER THOUGHTS RAISE such bedlam in her head that the number and even the purpose and recipient of the call all vanish within.

She can't get that boorish draftswoman, latent carrier of anti-Semitism and bestial hatred for the intelligentsia, out of her mind. The very thought of this potential pogrom-perpetrator causes Ophelia Feliksivna's fingers to twitch and spark unexpected rhythms from the telephone receiver. Among them are the march of the Pioneer Cubs—the one about "deep blue nights," the clickety-clack of a passing train, but it is the capricious jazz syncopes that dominate.

Because of the racket, Svitlana Zhuravlynchenko cannot wrestle down a simple sentence and puts her editing aside. Antonina Pavlivna glares at the receiver with hate. She can't recall, did she tell her husband to have Andriyko drink from the thermos once an hour or did she forget? And to stir up some hot milk with honey, butter, and baking soda at twelve o'clock. He knows he has to sweep the floor, wash the dishes, and peel the potatoes for supper. But about the thermos . . . will he remember?

The clatter is not allowing Zoyka Vereshchak either to work or to indulge in a decent bout of self-pity. Only Vitya Maliatko, having finally pulled out his quality papers, has fallen into a creative trance once more and takes no part in the general disquietude.

And yet, Ophelia Feliksivna tries to convince herself, no place is perfect. Here gifted and cultured people have to take abuse from common ruck. But there, as Ella writes, our Ph.D.'s spend eighteen hours a day behind the wheel of a cab. Here you're always dealing with a backward mentality, but at least everything's familiar and you're used to it. There you've got civilization, but is there really enough strength in her to begin anew? No, no, no. All is vanity and there are sinners everywhere.

The annoyed editors convey their feelings to one another with barely discernible movements of lips or eyes. Antonina Pavlivna suffers in silence. Svitlana coughs. Zoyka is gnawing at the office supplies. Finally even Vitya notices that hail is battering the house. He abandons his musings on magnetic lines of force in Van Gogh's paintings in midstream, and, looking about in alarm, beholds a consummate genre painting.

You wouldn't have to add or change a thing. Grab a pencil, jot down your first, still-quivering impressions, and then at home, with background music playing, apply oil to a canvas carefully primed beforehand, and create out of this idea, this abstraction, a perfectly material work of art. You don't like oils? Use gouache, or tempera, or watercolor. And then there's always collage. Or sculpture. How can they prattle on about the stylistic limitations of this or that medium? All you need is enough skill to reproduce that which the unjaundiced eye can see. For what is the manifest world, asks Vitya Maliatko, if not magnetic force lines of various voltages emanating from the present moment? And the same goes for all four elements! Catch them, hold them, love them, shape them!

But can Vitya Maliatko, locked up in his ivory tower, contemplate and replicate reality while his colleagues suffer from that very reality? He cannot. He therefore immediately casts his pencil to the floor, then his pen, then begins to reach for the state-purchased-with-hard-currency volume.

Zoyka stifles a chortle. The women are on his side. But no results as yet. Ophelia Feliksivna's eyes are turned inward. Her glasses, rather than maintain in her field of vision every detail of the behavior of her subordinates, perform a purely decorative function, that is, they sit astride the nose and adorn a marshmallow face.

The book of imported quality flies to the floor. It is followed by the telephone, hurled full force in one spasmodic movement by the terrified Ophelia Feliksivna. Simultaneously a primal scream is heard, comprised of all extant vowel phonemes.

The Door to the Room Opens, But Not Widely

TOMA'S HEAD JUTS OUT OF THE OPENING. TOMA IS ZOYKA'S tempestuous friend.

"Get over here! Got something to tell ya!" She alternately blinks her right, then her left eye.

Zoyka springs to her feet.

"Would you kindly tell your friend . . . !" Ophelia Feliksivna is annoyed. But Zoyka has whisked through the crack, so the admonishment that it is customary to say hello when one enters a room full of people ricochets against the closed door and takes a swipe at the co-workers.

"How coarse!" says Ophelia Feliksivna and shakes her head. She has just enough verve to formulate this simple, albeit several times repeated, conclusion.

The door handle clicks, the door keeps opening slightly, then banging shut. They hear Zoyka's eager voice, see one leg in green woolen tights, a black skirt made from a turned winter coat, the tip of a pug nose. Those who have been casting curious glances in that direction expect at any moment to see the other leg, the reddish coarsely woven sweater, and the girlish head. But Zoyka Vereshchak remembers something important and slams the door, disappearing from view altogether. As she stands in the corridor, she continues to tug at the handle, first increasing the opening, then reducing it to nil. At last she jumps back into the room, takes two steps, turns around, flings herself back to the door, screams "and don't you breathe a word!" and shakes her fist at Toma.

"Would you kindly tell your friend," Ophelia Feliksivna begins her rebuke, "that . . . "

"If you only knew, Ophelia Feliksivna," Zoyka Vereshchak says to her, "what she has just told me!"

Ophelia Feliksivna and Svitlana Zhuravlynchenko tense up in unison without ever having conspired to do so. Antonina Pavlivna freezes in the middle of a sentence. Vitya Maliatko twists his body into such a shape that according to certain laws of physics he will immediately fall down.

"But I'm not going to tell you," grins a radiant Zoyka and snuggles into her chair.

Ophelia Feliksivna pretends that Toma's news has in no way sparked her curiosity.

Antonina Pavlivna swiftly conquers the next paragraph. Svitlana Zhuravlynchenko lets out a disappointed huff. Vitya Maliatko does not smash the floor with the back of his head because he is anchored to the foot of the desk by the toe of his sturdy walking shoe.

The surviving remnants of the telephone call out from the stand. It's Lupova, head of the Department of Scientific and Technical Information, asking to see Ophelia Feliksivna.

Aaahh!—Svitlana Zhuravlynchenko Stretches Her Young Body

HER ARMS REACH PASSIONATELY TO THE CEILING, HER HANDS link in the bond of unbreakable friendship, and she completes the exercise with a heartfelt sigh. Now, if only Ophelia, instead of returning with new assignments, would crawl back from Lupova saying, "You don't have to do another thing. Hang around till the break, girls, have lunch, and then head over to HIVTS for a concert. The union, behind the backs of the administration, has made secret arrangements with the Entertainment Bureau to invite the latest Leningrad pop group." HIVTS has a huge hall; they normally herd all NIIAA, NIIUP, and NIITS employees there on the eve of a revolutionary holiday. But when it comes to meeting the real needs of the workers, forget it!

Today, however, Svitlana has another reason for sadness.

Last night her mother-in-law dropped by and announced: You're not looking after Dimochka properly, he's running around snot-nosed, you don't make soups, you don't stock up on groceries, you're neglecting your poor husband Vitalik. Svitlana bursts out crying, dashes into the bathroom, runs the water, sobs, blows her nose, washes her face, and would like to come back out already, but she is choking from insult. And so, rather than blast the intruder with an icy stare as would befit the lady of the house, she bites into her finger and sheds hot tears on the cut.

"One could almost assume," whispers Svitlana, "that you

took good care of *your* son! You once told me yourself how revolting it was to wash his diapers. And not even the ones with poop, just the damp ones!" And when she had to empty his potty it would turn her insides right out. She told me herself, nobody dragged it out of her! Said her husband would come home from work and harness himself to the sink until night scraping baby shit off the gauze.

But why doesn't her husband, Vitalik, defend her? How long can you be a mama's boy?

At night, little Dima is barely asleep when he's on top of her, he wants to make up. It makes no difference to him what she's feeling, whether she's hurt or maybe already sleeping. He's dreamed up something under his blanket there and is now demanding some weird position. Svitlana silently fights him off, trying not to wake up her son.

"Am I that repulsive?" he asks. "Is it really so hard for you?"

Svitlana doesn't answer, but doesn't resist either. Vitalik can be stubborn, but having surmounted opposition, he muddles through wearily and not for very long. Before falling asleep he reproaches her for coldness, indifference, poor housekeeping and child-rearing, and reminds her that the women he dated before marrying her were capable of reaching orgasm ahead of him.

Svitlana defends herself, saying that the man, too, must involve himself in the process and thus advance the goal of mutual harmony. All the manuals say this. "I'm trying as hard as I can as it is!" she sobs. "Here, in the kitchen, at work. I could be in graduate school right now! My diploma was once commended as one of the best and most academically promising!"

But, she admits to herself, down deep I realize the issue here is not intellect, but the fact that I am probably completely frigid when it comes to men. I have never known this higher feeling called orgasm. I don't understand, even, what kind of joy it could be. And without orgasm my life is destined for eternal grayness, there is no release, and my work and my family suffer.

"Help me," she whispers quietly, and strokes her husband's back, down the spine, from the narrow neck down lower and lower to the furry buttocks. But Vitalik is fast asleep.

Antonina Pavlivna Swiftly Dispenses with Her Portion of the NIIAA Annual Report

FASTIDIOUSLY, LIKE A BAYONET, HER PENCIL FOLLOWS LINE after line of chancellery prose, finding a stylistic gaffe here, the absence of a required comma there. Oh, if only she could squeeze out forty-five (perhaps fifty!) pages today. Fifty-five or sixty would be even better! And after that come seven sheets of graphs, and following those a hodgepodge of tables, footnotes, and the final wisps of a conclusion. So if Andriyko gets better in the next day or two and she doesn't have to take sick leave, then tomorrow she can launch a full-scale attack and deliver a death blow to the whole report, and then by the end of the week finish darning Volodya's sock and even take a peek at the novel that a neighbor gave her last Sunday. Because Zoyka Vereshchak, and now Svitlana Zhuravlynchenko, too, are falling behind: It seems they want to delve deep into the gently flowing waters of the saga that springs from the dense Siberian forests on the eve of the Japanese campaign and that meanders, not bypassing a single significant occurrence, all the way to the lukewarm present.

The authors of the television film boasting the same title have changed everything, as it turns out, falsified all the events, threw out some of the plot lines (for example, Zina's love for Prokhor), introduced corrections in others, modernized them, and streamlined the whole thing into one bewildering mess!

But God forbid that this dry cough should become mucous and advance from the unresistant trachea to the bronchi and from there on to the child's delicate lungs. While Ophelia Feliksivna absorbs Lupova's directive, Antonina Pavlivna sits herself down at the telephone and dials her home number.

Volodya picks up right away.

Andriy had breakfast, took his medicine, he's now lying down, reading. There is no draft in the room, Volodya has not taken his temperature, he remembers about the milk, and asks that she not remind him for the tenth time. The doctor came by. No, she did not prescribe any pills. Raspberry tea, mustard plasters, honey, that's all she said. She didn't mention compresses. Well, what do they know anyway?!

Antonina Pavlivna wants to speak with her son.

"Great, Mom," Andriy is glad to talk. "You know . . . Yes, yes, I drank it! Did you know . . . You're not listening! Good. Then listen if you say you're interested. Do you know how to tell albino rabbits from nonalbino ones? Do you? Give up? You have to look at their eyes! If they're very red, it's an albino. No, I didn't make that up. I read it in that book that Dad bought for me. So, will you remember? The first thing you do is look at their eyes. All right, here he is. Da-a-ad!"

"When are you getting home?" Volodya asks. "Go straight over to Lupova, tell her: Either give me half a day now or I'll be off all week on sick leave. Tell her just like that. What do you mean 'I can't'? What is this 'busy'? What time have you got there? Fine. I'm giving you twenty minutes. They won't die without you. Love you. Okay. Twenty minutes!"

The first commentary on the overheard conversation comes from Zoyka Vereshchak.

"Guys are useless!" she says. "Can't do a thing on their own. If I had a husband, I'd make him do all the housework, I'd just supervise and hedonize. Hedonize and supervise."

Svitlana Zhuravlynchenko is interested in the child's temperature and mentions that under no circumstances should you try to bring it down, because a fever is an indication that the body has mobilized all its resources to fight the flu antibodies.

"But it's not the flu that he's got, it's a cough," explains Antonina Pavlivna. "Last year we consulted a professor and he diagnosed exudative diathesis. Build up his immunity until he grows out of it, he told us."

"Too bad he doesn't have asthma," says Zoyka. "Because asthma is now very successfully treated in salt caves. I read it yesterday in *The Worker*."

"You're a dreamer," Svitlana tells her. "Try getting a pass to one of those."

"Oh no, no caves!" gasps Antonina Pavlivna. "We'll apply compresses every night, and we'll even get suction cups . . . "

"Ooh, I wouldn't mind hanging around a cave for a while," confesses Zoyka.

"You're taking things a little far," they tell her. "You should go demand that they give you a place to live instead."

"Oh!" Zoyka turns red and hides her eyes. "Not with my luck!"

She buries herself in the dictionary and covers her face with her hands, so that nobody in the whole world would guess why Toma had come to see her. Because Toma did not simply pop by for a chat, but rather in the strictest confidence informed her friend that tomorrow she, Zoyka Vereshchak, would be assigned living space.

"Just Don't You Dare . . . ," Toma Had Said. "Not a Word!"

"ARE YOU KIDDING?!" ZOYKA CROSSES HER HEART. "YOU think I'm stupid?"

Although, on the other hand, she wouldn't mind spilling

everything to her co-workers. But she is a little bit, or rather, quite frightened of this, to be completely honest. Although she'd really like to . . . But what if everything were to suddenly fall through? What if someone goes out and lets it slip somewhere ? Or reports it? Or puts a hex on her?

Now, if she had her own one-room apartment and not a creaky cast-iron bed and night table at the dorm, would she be afraid of anything? Or anybody? Never!

Like, let's say, Ninka Pikhota from the personnel section walks up to her (the one down in the lobby every morning compiling the criminally late list), or else Woodnov, head of the Foreign Contacts Group, or Lupova, or even the director himself. If she had at that time even a tiny, matchbox-size, but separate individual hole in the wall, Zoyka would give them all such an earful they'd still be quaking in their boots!

But before sending them all to hell, she'd sob bitterly and long, because for some reason everyone seems to pick on her, a single, lonely girl from the backwoods of the neighboring county. And besides, under the present unjust conditions, who could repress such an outburst of injured feeling? Somebody, probably very cruel, who carries a warehouse lock in his chest instead of a heart.

Her aunt was absolutely right when she said to her: "Until you have a key and until you turn that key and walk inside (screw the renovations!) and turn both dead bolts and hook up the chain—but if you really want to make sure, then it wouldn't hurt to attach a wide metal plate with two heavy screws—until that moment you can't afford to relax about this thing."

Zoyka's aunt receives a well-deserved pension and helps out her niece any way she can with advice. She lives pretty close by.

"And what if they don't give me an apartment?" Zoyka asks her.

"How can they not give you an apartment?" asks the aunt

in amazement. "You go up to them and reveal how much continuous service you've logged, remind them that you're here on the postgraduate distribution of professional cadre quota, that you have never flinched from any duty whatsoever, that you could have finished school a year sooner if you hadn't been sent off to the sanatorium for treatment in grade 6."

"And what if they say, 'We've got a waiting list dozens of years long? And not just one, several! One for the war heroes, one for the invalids, obviously, and another for the promising youth . . . '"

"Promising youth!" The aunt launches an assault on Zoyka Vereshchak. "Youth can wait! Take a look at what's going on around you! Yesterday I go to pay the electric bill, I get in line, stand there waiting, when suddenly, out of nowhere, this painted-up hussy floats by . . . "

"But what if they refuse?" insists the niece.

"Well, then you tell them," the aunt pulls back her ash-speckled shoulders, "you tell them: Do you know who I am? From what kind of family? Do you know who my aunt is, who her father was? Well, do you? Then read the book *Flaming Smoke* by Vaillis and Krutykh. Or take a ride down to our regional museum, and more concretely, to the stand where certain artifacts are displayed, namely, the riding breeches, medal, and security pass of Pervomay Ivanovych Vereshchak. And as far as the distinctions bestowed on my first aunt, well, you tell them, there is an oral commitment from Comrade Budka, the museum director, that she will be granted a special corner in the peaceful coexistence section. So let this institute commission of yours stop squawking and shut up!"

This reassures Zoyka. She puts the dictionary aside, looks around at who's doing what, and waits for everyone to start tugging at her—come on, tell us what Toma was whispering to you in the hall, open up, you know it's dishonest to keep secrets from your fellow workers!

Ophelia Feliksivna Enters the Room with a Red File
and Issues an Unexpected Command

SHE SAYS: "PUT AWAY THE INSTITUTE ANNUAL REPORT! WE have a new job. We're editing the materials from Liahushenko's department."

"What about the report?" The women are taken aback. "We were to get through it by the end of the week! All that work! There's only two days' worth left! How can we just leave everything in mid-sentence?! And why Liahushenko? Where's the sense in this? Please, explain!"

"Work on the report," explains Ophelia Feliksivna, "has been postponed until Friday."

"But we won't be able to do it in a day!" they tell her. "How many pages in the Liahushenko?"

"About two hundred plus."

"Are they out of their minds?!" wail Antonina Pavlivna and Svitlana Zhuravlynchenko.

"We'll have to," Ophelia Feliksivna concludes, and adds that it has come to her attention that the ministry is holding a competition for the best department in the institutions under its jurisdiction. Since Deputy Director Sapyolkin is retiring, it was decided that the subsector entrusted to his command would not be entering the competition this time. Wasting no time, the up-and-coming junior scholars Liahushenko and Brovarsky leaped into the existing vacuum with their people. At today's planning session Liahushenko pulled Lomaka and Doktorchuk over to his side, and they succeeded in wresting recognition for Liahushenko's team as superior in the development of progressive methodology. That's why by tomorrow their papers, properly compiled, edited, and brought to order in a manner befitting documents from the department chosen to serve as the calling card and mirror of the entire NIIAA, must be lying on the minister's desk. That's all there is to it."

"But that's absurd!" exclaim the editors. "Look at it yourself. To properly edit anything like this . . . "

"Oh," sighs Ophelia Feliksivna, "why are you telling me this? As if I can't see it myself!"

It is difficult to doubt the sincerity of her words, because this time Lupova has dolloped out so much work that no matter how wisely and equitably Ophelia Feliksivna were to divide it among her younger colleagues, some of this stale manufactured prose was going to end up on her desk, too.

"What do they think they're doing?!" The women engage in a little free thinking. "Why is it always like this in our country?! Lies and liars everywhere. Always pulling the wool over our eyes. Not even a whiff of justice. Who needs the work we do? We're just ruining our eyes! If at least there was hope for something better! Or faith . . . "

"What faith! Who believes in anything anymore? In what? In whom?"

"How can you believe if you can see right through them? I see through every last one of them!"

"Me, too!"

"Me, too!"

"Me, too!"

"Me, too," confesses Zoyka Vereshchak, although the squeeze with the Liahushenko report does not affect her personally.

"I finally saw the light," she tells them, "after that lottery incident. Remember? Nelka got them. She gets rid of six tickets and no way can she sell any more. She comes running to me. Help, she says. I take the tickets and head straight over to Kroutko, he was the Komsomol rep then. Who gave these to you? I ask him. The district party committee, he says. I phone there. Is this a voluntary thing, I ask, or not? Voluntary, they say. Wonderful, I thank them very much. So I ask around, who wants some? No takers. I collected the money, counted it up to make sure, packed it up with the remaining tickets, and turned the whole thing in. Next day, *scandaloso* like you wouldn't believe! They call an extraordinary meeting, the party secretary is demoted, I get a reprimand. If I didn't have family, I would have spit the whole truth right in their faces! But this way, if they were to put me away, there'd be a black spot against my aunt and her whole biography. I just have no right to do something like that to her."

"My husband's grandfather is one of those, too," Antonina Pavlivna remembers. "He wasn't even sixteen when he took part in the storming of . . . "

"And mine wasn't yet fifteen, and he was somebody . . . !"

"Mine supervised a center!"

"My grandma saw Comrade Stakhanov!"

"Yes," the rest jump in, "things were simple then. Not like now."

"And there was such commitment to ideals!"

"Yeah, but just look at what they did to them!"

"Who? To whom?"

"To the ideals! You know yourselves who."

"Yes! Yes! It's horrible!" the women cry out joyfully, one ahead of the other. "Look what it's come to! Everything's rotting in this country, falling apart. They've shattered illusions! Liquidated the stimuli! Clouded us in deception. But they can have everything: special hospitals, special stores where you can get anything you want. We should all get together and tell them: Enough is enough! We will not edit your Liahushenko! Because this is too much! Exploitation! If we all rise up, what can they do? Oh, how I hate them all!"

"Me, too!"

"Me, too!"

"Me, too!"

Someone on the Other Side of the Door Abruptly Yanks It Toward Him

The windowpanes rattle against the frame, the frame hits the cactus, the cactus wobbles, ready to fall and hurt itself, but is intercepted in the nick of time by Vitya Maliatko, whose reward is to sit and pull cactus needles from his palms for some time thereafter.

"Excuse me, please, where can I find . . . " they hear, but do not yet see Rozzhestvenik, supervisor of the ERA Duplicating corps, "Tamara Zakharivna?"

Before entering a dwelling or establishment (his own or someone else's, no matter), he likes to linger by the door for a moment, sniff about furtively, stalk the air in quest of suspicious sounds, and then spend a little time mulling over the received signals. Just like now, for example: shouts, yells bouncing off the walls. But hell knows who exactly is doing what to whom and why, you know, you just never know. That's why it's always a good idea not to thrust yourself in too boldly and to keep that door crack nice and narrow so there are no surprises.

"Tamara Zakharivna Lupova," the response reaches him, "does not have her office here. How many times do we have to tell you? She's down the hall."

"Oh." Feeling a little bolder, Rozzhestvenik squeezes half his torso into the suspicious room, takes note of the postures, furnishings, the facial expressions of those present. "Sorry to bother you."

"All the best!" they wish him.

"Did you hear," he asks, "what the radio said today?"

"The radio's talking to you? Which radio is this?" Vitya Maliatko is curious.

"Ours!" Rozzhestvenik informs him with pleasure. "Not the one that's been poisoning your mind since birth! Ours! From the PA system! Soviet."

"Ivan Havrylovych," Vitya goes on the offensive, "you're a war veteran, right?"

"Yeah."

"Which front were you on?"

Vitya is badgering Rozzhestvenik, because he knows that Rozzhestvenik spent four years of World War II maintaining vigilance in peaceful China in the remote case of a perfidious attack by imperial Japan.

The situation was desperate. The samurai were paying two thousand per head of each of our officers (well his, too, obviously). You had to take a gun to the toilet. Plus two Chinese bodyguards. But they, the Chinese, that is, always had exceptional regard for us Russians. If it weren't for old Nikita, we'd still be best friends.

"Which front? I'll tell you which front," Rozzhestvenik tells Vitya Maliatko. "They've filled their heads with Voice of This and Voice of That, especially the youth, and they're making a whorehouse out of this country!"

"Well, what can be done?" they ask him. "How can we fight these tendencies?"

"The way that you fight them," advises Rozzhestvenik, "is that you don't get too bloody smart!"

There's a rumor going around NIIAA that Rozzhestvenik is a rich peasant's son, that the gypsies stole him from the cradle but couldn't get him to learn either to steal horses or to play the guitar, and turned him in to a Suvorov military school. But of course that's just a tall tale. The Suvorov boarding schools appeared only after the war, and by that time Rozzhestvenik had risen to the rank of captain. Later he exchanged his stripes for a director's chair allocating housing on behalf of the district executive committee, continued in the managerial line by pursing a career in supply distribution, and wound up, finally, in a research institute, where he oversees duplication technology.

"So what do you suggest, specifically?" The women insist on an answer.

"What I suggest is this." Passion enflames Rozzhestvenik. "If they put away about two or three, the rest would be meek as mice!"

"So that's what's on your mind!" Room 507 erupts. "Like in 1937! Let's purge the faithful party cadres! Let's have more repressions! And what would you say if they came and picked you up in the middle of the night?!"

"Let them take me!" Rozzhestvenik puffs out his chest and would ruffle his feathers if he had any. "If I deserve it, I'll take my medicine! There'll be less of a mess!"

"Bravo!" applaud the editors and translators. "Stepped right into your own trap. You're absolutely right! Bravo!"

"What did I say?" Rozzhestvenik backs off. "I didn't say anything! You're the ones sitting around here dreaming up insurgencies!"

"Weren't you looking for Tamara Zakharivna?" they remind him.

"I wasn't looking for anyone!" Rozzhestvenik's feelings are hurt. He closes the door gently, but very tightly, as if pulling a noose until all breathing stops, and he disappears from view.

"Made a mistake, poor guy! Got the wrong room!" Hisses nip at his heels. "Eavesdropping!"

"I got so scared!"

"Pretending he's just a fool!"

"What do you think . . . "

"He stopped in to spy on us!"

"Stool pigeon!"

"Here you have a perfect example of that gray mass thanks to which, moreover, with the acquiescence of which, all the grave crimes are committed!"

"What do you think . . . "

"A guy like that does well in any regime!"

"Rozzhestvenik is a man of the System—its product and its maker simultaneously. Here's the true embodiment of evil! All the Hitlers in the world couldn't hold a candle to a guy like him!"

"We're defenseless!"

"What do you think, could he . . . "

"Jerk!"

"And they control us! God, what kind of place do we live in?!"

"What do you think, could he have heard our conversation?"

The ring of the telephone cuts the air.

"Hello!" says Ophelia Feliksivna. "Hello! May I . . . "

At the sound of her strained voice, the party on the other end hangs up.

Everyone suddenly becomes very still, their breath knocked out. They do their best to convey an aura of silent indifference, as if a moment ago not one of them had offered half-baked or bombastic pronouncements.

"I Should Have Kept My Mouth Shut," Ophelia Feliksivna Tells Herself

ALL PRESENT SILENTLY AGREE WITH HER.

"And what exactly is your problem, you of all people?" Antonina Pavlivna chastises herself. "Do you not have a family, or something? Who's going to look after them should something, God forbid, knock wood, happen to you?"

"You don't need a Rozzhestvenik around here," Svitlana Zhuravlynchenko assures herself, "to get out-lied and sold down the river. And the worst thing is that you'll never even know who did it."

Ophelia Feliksivna stubbornly strokes page 1 of the Liahushenko papers. "No!" she tries to convince someone. "No, this country's finished, that's been clear for a long time now. Nothing good is ever going to happen here. As long as the people are the way they are. And the circumstances.

Metamorphoses were possible, perhaps, in Virgil's time. Or, rather, in Ovid's. Who, tell me, who, when, and how will we ever be able to reeducate them? And how many years, or generations, or centuries will it take?"

Vitya Maliatko makes a few doodles, on the basis of which one can see immediately that he has trouble drawing people. And that's not only because he doesn't have enough practice yet, or because he's never studied this craft and it's only been a few years since he decided to become an artist. The reason lies elsewhere. Even his amateur eye can see what a fatal effect people have on natural lines of force. How they distort them with their persistent voracious outbursts. How they are all weighed down by something essentially human, shaky and unstable, something that's not always easy to find words for. "Because," Vitya looks around, "what can you extract for the purposes of art from these indoor, multifigure, anthropomorphic, eight-hour-a-day compositions? Perhaps only the pettiness of their 'I'll scratch your back, you'll scratch mine' relations? Is this worth the trouble of making sketches, stretching canvas over a frame, priming it, and so on? And what if I suddenly discover that I have no talent? No, I'll work on landscapes for starters. Nature will never lead you astray."

"Sure!" Zoyka Vereshchak's eyes blaze from out of her nook. "Everyone has an individual living space assignment but me! You call that justice?! Svitlana's in-laws put up money for a co-op. Antonina Pavlivna, Vitya Maliatko— they all have somewhere to live. Since the death of her parents Ophelia Feliksivna has occupied two adjacent rooms and a hallway by herself with a complete set of Brockhaus and Efron. And over her grand piano there's a framed watercolor, an original from the last century, that shows how a Berber savage, mounted on an steed, has cut off the head of a colonial officer and is brandishing it by the locks. If she spent a little time in my communal quarters, she'd lose her appetite for pictures like that!"

Like last night, Zoyka's roommate, Valentyna, played records all evening, and when Zoyka threatened to go to the commandant, she answered: I have a full legal right to play them until eleven o'clock. Exactly at eleven Zoyka turned out the lights, because, incidentally, Valentyna deliberately burns a lot of electricity and heists Zoyka's food from the fridge, those things that are hard to prove (sour cream, for example, or soup, although Zoyka hasn't made soup for a while, it takes too much time). So then Valentyna got into bed and kept singing those same songs until her snoring took over. And Zoyka had barely closed her eyes when she started hissing and scratching the windowpane with a greasy fork until dawn. In the morning Zoyka asks her: Valentyna, why do you do this? Why do I do what? her roommate gapes. And when Zoyka explained it all to her, she parted her jowls and let out very many filthy words, the true meaning of which remains a hot mystery for Zoyka to this day.

Ophelia Feliksivna is calling Antonina Pavlivna to the phone. It's Volodya.

"Well?!" he says. "Why are you still there? It's almost one. Did you get off? What do you mean 'almost'? You can't tell them? I see. Go to Ophelia, go to Lupova, go to whoever you want, but take care of it. If there's no bus, take a cab, because I already told them at work that I'm leaving. Okay. I'm waiting."

"Ophelia Feliksivna!" Antonina Pavlivna assumes a pleading posture.

But the boss has already figured everything out and, jumping in ahead of her, asks the editors how many pages each has done. A quick tempo is good, she lectures, but don't forget about quality either. Because where there's a scramble, there's a jumble, and then there's always, each and every time, missed commas, clumsy syntax, gross lapses in meaning. Don't forget we're dealing with the ministerial level here!

"My son!" Rather than spell out the essence of the issue

logically and concisely, Antonina Pavlivna can only discharge broken fragments of pain. "I'll be so careful! Let me go!"

"Well, first of all," Ophelia Feliksivna elucidates, "it's forbidden . . . "

"I won't sleep all night! I'll bring the whole text complete tomorrow morning!"

"Well, first of all, you should sleep at night . . . "

"The child's health! My husband's only till noon! Can't you understand!"

"First of all," Ophelia Feliksivna raises her voice, "I, unlike some other people, do understand. There's no need to make me into a tyrant. And I would also ask you (and this, by the way, concerns everybody!) not to mix your domestic problems and your personal life with your work. There is such a thing as a professional ethic, which states: If I have come to work, then I have to *work*. That's first of all. And second, let your husband spend some time looking after the child, too. What if the director suddenly asks: Oh, where's Smyrnova? Who let her take time off? This, by the way, demonstrates a fundamental lack of regard on your part for the entire sector!"

Antonina Pavlivna bites her lower lip and sits down.

"If you were out in the West," says Ophelia Feliksivna, "do you know what your boss . . . "

But she stops herself in time.

Volodya phones again.

"You haven't left?" his crazed voice lashes Antonina Pavlivna. "What are you trying to do, drive me nuts? What do you mean, you'll try? What new assignment? How can you do this? We agreed! I've screwed everyone at work now. You want me to leave all this or something? This is what you do . . . You tell this Desdemona of yours . . . Don't you 'quiet' me! Let them all hear! Julietta Dobermanivna, give me a break! I want you here in twenty minutes! . . . Andriy! Put it down! Put the thermos back where it belongs! Get down! What did I just say! Did you hear me? I'll leave all this! Why don't you say anything? Hello! If you're not, I repeat, in fifteen minutes . . . Hey, put it down! Andriy! Oh, you're going to get . . . "

The last thing Antonina Pavlivna hears coming out of the receiver before the click is the peal of shattering glass, yelps, a slap, and the piercing cry of a child.

"What is it? What's happened?" Antonina Pavlivna's fingertips grow cold. Andriy wanted to drink, tipped the thermos, cut his hand? Crawled to the top of the cupboard and fell down? Walked up to the stove and knocked the kettle of boiling water all over himself? Started playing with the thermometer, broke it, lapped up the balls of mercury with his tongue, and swallowed them?

She keeps dialing home and getting the same alarming beeps.

I Can't Take It Anymore!

This thought flares up not only in Antonina Pavlivna's mind. For one temporally insignificant yet unbearably exquisite moment it permeates all five souls. And these souls, strange as it may seem, surrender to it unconditionally, without asking what is this strange thing, where did it come from, where will it go and why. During this communal moment of truth, each one has just enough time to ask him- or herself: Who am I? How did I end up here? Is this what my life should be? Is the load I'm pulling really mine? Because if we were to first stand up and then take a good look around, we would see a colorful joyful world swarming with life all about us. Why are we rotting alive in this stench? It's contemptible!

Why am I not at home? Antonina Pavlivna has just enough time to ask herself. With the ones I love and who are dear to me? Who in this world will gain from the fact that I have neglected them and spent years reading reams of someone else's repellent prose? I must drop everything and get out of here now. To the place where I am driven by my feminine heart.

Vitya Maliatko grabs his tousled head. Am I not, he asks himself, one of the select few? Am I not a favorite of the gods? Because I see and I feel not like the others. Why the devil am I sitting here decomposing? Pissing my life away! In those five days that the government robs me of each week I could create countless masterpieces!

I was made for happiness! Svitlana Zhuravlynchenko finally realizes. To spread out my wings and fly. For the intense experience. But they have robbed me of that which is a right and absolute necessity for every woman. A duty, even. How much of that full-bodied life have I got left, anyway? And I have still not known the ultimate joy!

Action! You must act! Ophelia Feliksivna decides once and for all. I am talented, cultured, and not that old yet. HERE I will perish. I must get OUT THERE! It's the only way! THERE the air is purer, the food is better. And the general level! The service! The medical care! It's like heaven and earth! I'll write and get them to put in the sponsor forms right away. Adjustment will be difficult, but that's only fair. The subsequent decent life will compensate for everything. No one's asked to come back yet.

Freedom, like a gust of fresh air, unexpectedly burst into Room 507 and so roused everyone that even Zoyka, who has no particular place to rush home to, is overwhelmed with joy and solemnly swears to clean and polish every inch of her future abode and to put flowers in every corner.

Half an hour before the break, much to his own surprise, he slams down the quality volume (still open at the section dealing with psychological aspects of obsession with macrobiotics), rips his shabby coat off the hook, and makes for the door.

The most creative years of my life are now! the thought suddenly strikes him. If I am to define my style as an artist, if there really is to be a new life for me, then it must begin right away. Why put it off? I'll drop off my letter of resignation another time.

"What's with you? Lunch is coming up!" Everyone is surprised. "You'll get your name in the black book! They'll stop you at the exit!"

Vitya places a hand on his lower belly and without bending his knees makes quick jerking movements sideways toward the door, all the while demonstrating how he has summoned his last resources for the control of bodily functions.

"Come back!" Zoyka shouts after him. But instead of a farewell, he once more shows his face, contorted from stomach cramps, and disappears.

"A guy like that will make it anywhere," says Ophelia Feliksivna.

The telephone sounds the alarm from the stand. Woodnov, head of the Foreign Contacts Group, has succumbed to a need to say something to Vitya Maliatko.

"You know," answers Svitlana Zhuravlynchenko, "he just stepped out . . . "

"Has he been gone long?"

"No, literally one second . . . "

"Very well, then." Woodnov cuts her off and hangs up. He keeps track of all his underlings' transgressions, but in Vitya he has a special interest. His old friend Vankhadlo (they both started out once upon a time in the same attentive and well-informed institution) has a daughter who's going to need a job in about six months. She's a clever girl in her last year of foreign languages and, like the rest of them, would like to dedicate her life to the travel-abroad line of work. Her father doesn't have quite enough stars yet to parachute her into one of those free-enterprise countries, so it would be best if the girl got into a research institute for now, not too far from daddy's watchful eye. That position that Vitya Maliatko holds, for example, wouldn't be too bad. He's useless anyway, whether to the institution or to the state. While for her we can find some gentle assignment in the Komsomol and with time organize the necessary recommendations. And then, God willing, something may pop up in the genre of international friendship. How can you not help out an old buddy? Vankhadlo is the reliable sort. It may choke him, but he'll always pay you back.

"Oh!" Says Zoyka, For She So Wants to Share Her Exciting News

THE WOMEN ARE QUIET, EACH IN HER OWN WORLD.

"If it wasn't for Toma," she admits out loud, "if it wasn't for her connections . . . "

But nobody's in any great hurry to lend an ear.

"So, as I was saying"—Zoyka is hurt by the whole world—"you can live or you can die, nobody gives a damn! That's the way it is in this country . . . "

"What? How? When? Who's dying?" Her startled colleagues wake up.

"Nobody's dying," a delighted Zoyka explains carefully. "But somebody's going to be getting an apartment!"

"Who? Where? When? How?"

Not right away, but after a long sadistic pause Zoyka announces, "Me. Today. I'm getting one. An apartment!"

"You're kidding!?" The women can't believe it. "How do you know? What kind of apartment? Who told you? Come on, spit it out! Just imagine, sitting there and not saying a word to us!"

"I had no idea myself," Zoyka defends herself. "Here I am working quietly, translating, when suddenly Toma . . . "

"Did the commission approve it?"

"Apparently so . . . "

"Our internal trade union commission, or has it gone to the district level? Has the assignment been made or are you just on the final list? What is it, an efficiency unit? Institute housing? Regional jurisdiction or city? What did Toma say?"

"I didn't ask!"

"Well, you better go find out and tell us. And in the meantime, knock wood."

Knock, knock knock! Zoyka raps the table.

"And spit. No, not like that, over your left shoulder! And throw some salt over, too. Here, I've got some right here. Well, how about that, good old Zoyka, didn't breathe a word, like an old paratrooper! You'd better have a bottle in here tomorrow."

"I don't drink!"

"But we do!"

Room 507 puts away all its paperwork and proceeds to rejoice loudly and sincerely over Zoyka's good fortune.

"Quiet, quiet, you guys," Zoyka waves her arms. "Someone might walk in."

"Let them! Let the whole world know!"

"Oh no, better not. I've got this ringing in my ear as it is."

"Which one? If it's the right ear you'll get good news."

"What about the left ear?"

"The left is bad news"

"What if it's both?"

"I don't know about both. But I can tell you about an itchy palm or if you drop your change. That I know from personal experience."

"I've heard about an itchy palm," Zoyka says. "And about if your nose itches. And the bridge of your nose. And black cats."

"The cat story's a lie," they tell her. "Superstition. The same goes for the number thirteen. I've had a black cat for three years. And my mother-in-law has a . . . "

"Aah!" Zoyka straightens out her soft shoulders. "I'm going to walk into my new place, and the first thing I'll do is lock the door! . . . "

"Forget about locking!" she is told. "There's not going to be a lock. People get their permit, walk in, and all they see is . . . "

"I got myself a lock ages ago," boasts Zoyka, "and a spice rack made in Germany. Came across it by absolute chance. Very nice little drawers, too, they thought of everything: salt, pepper, ginger, cloves, vanilla, coriander . . . "

"You'd better hold off with that," they warn her. "You know what kind of apartments they give out to mere mortals these days? When you walk in, there's nothing but bare walls. The floor's warped. Wallpaper's gone. The parquet floor's still glued down here and there, but mostly not. And forget about faucets. You're lucky, if you'll pardon me for saying so, if someone hasn't left you shit piles all over the place."

"So I'll let a few lovers stay there first," Zoyka tells them. "They can do my renovations. You say you love me, I'll tell them, so now you can show me how much."

"And where are you going to find all these lovers, my dear?" they ask.

"What do you mean? Same place as everybody else. I just didn't need any so far. Didn't even have a closet to take them to. But now it's a different story. I'll spread rumors around town that I've become a loose woman . . . "

"And what if a whole horde stampedes over?"

"I'll run away! I'll jump into my legally registered apartment, lock the door, and say that there's nobody home."

"And what if they ask who's that lying to them through the keyhole?"

"I'll tell them it's the radio."

"Don't fool around with that stuff," they warn her. "You know what kinds of things are going on all over the city! It's not just fly-by-night lovers who are winding up as corpses, but legally married husbands, too."

"How does something like that happen? Tell me."

"Gladly."

Once Upon a Time There Lived a Woman. She Worked as a Biologist.

SHE LOVED ANIMALS. SHE GETS A NEW APARTMENT. HER HUS-band takes some time off work to fix up the floors. And before that he borrowed a planer from his friend and honed the blades really well. His neighbor's friend had a stand at the market, a little workbench where they sharpened knives, all kinds of scissors, meat grinders. Even nail clippers. His name was Kostiantyn, if I'm not mistaken. That night the woman comes home. No, no, it wasn't Kostiantyn! Mykola! Kolka! Anyway, she unlocks the door, calmly steps into her legally registered apartment, and gasps: Her husband's lying in the middle of the floor. Naked. With his head split open. And a kitten meowing at his feet. Her friend at work once gave it to her. I've got six of them, she said. If you don't take it, I'll have to drown it. And it was winter then, a real cold spell! Well, the first thing she does is call the police. They rush him over to emergency. One thing leads to another, and in the end he comes to in the recovery room and explains exactly what happened. He started stripping the varnish. First he had breakfast. Didn't drink. I have a rule, he says, first I work, then I get to that business. And even then it has to be around a table, with food, for a special occasion, in the company of friends (and I always pay my fair share, of course). So there he is working away. He starts to sweat. Takes off his shirt, his blue jogging pants, undershirt, boxers—absolutely everything. The kitten's keeping close by, it notices this man is scraping the floor and his whole body's shaking, everything's swinging back and forth, especially between his legs. The kitten gets interested, then leaps!—and sinks its claws right into to you-know-what. The man lets out a yowl, jumps up, bangs his head against the radiator, and for a time body and soul parted ways.

"So you see," everyone tells Zoyka Vereshchak, "what a serious business renovating a new apartment can be!"

"Oh, I don't need for anything like that to happen," Zoyka says in alarm. "I'll settle for no wallpaper and no linoleum, as long as it's a place of my own. It can even be without windows. As long as it has a roof, walls, a door, and a strong, stiff, simple mechanical lock. Don't tell me I don't deserve that much!"

"You certainly do," they tell her.

"When I was still in third year," Zoyka waves her arms, "I went to the German Democratic Republic for two weeks! Even in NIIAA I've seen many very highly placed individuals—like when, during a conference, I was entrusted to deliver papers from a working meeting to the deputy minister. And it wasn't because there was no one else in the director's office at the time! I remember old man Kysil sitting in there with his Order of Labor medals and huge teeth dripping with saliva, and then there was old lady Krishtopenko, and Petya the photographer, who used to work in the mines and then took some courses and took over the lab. That's because he was kind of in the party, although he sure was a boozer, the likes of which you don't run into very often. But out of all of them they chose me!"

"Zoy, hey Zoy," they're teasing her now, "tell us about how you translated for the director when he had to call Dresden."

"Leipzig," Zoyka corrects them.

"What's the difference?! Tell us what happened!"

"Well," Zoyka recalls, "that day I come in to work ten minutes early, so he'd see that I'm not the type to be late. And there's the director sitting under the Lenin portrait with the telephone receiver wedged between his shoulder and his ear. He's talking to the ministry, making notes with his right hand, punching the switchboard keys with his left, calling the secretary over in sign language so as not to waste even a second. He gives the following order: Kindly go to the library and take out on my personal card the latest American books on cybernetics, a documentary spy novel, and a collection of Smeliakov poems. That's what I call a real artist!"

"So what did you think of him?" her colleagues keep teasing. "What's he built like, his torso, biceps, thighs . . . You've got a real eye for these things, Zoy . . . "

"Well, I didn't undress him!" Zoyka is happy to play along.

"Oh ho ho! Ah ha ha! Such modesty, listen to her!"

"What did I say?!"

"Now we know what's really on your mind!"

The women remember how they've seen the director dressed in things other than a suit. In the springtime the whole NIIAA staff was taken out to the fields, first to plant cucumbers and later to weed them. That time the director, dressed in his blue-and-white Olympic jersey and sneakers, infused them with the true spirit of socialist competition and hoed to the end of his row first. The institute's party boss came in second, the trade union boss third . . . And what about that Volunteer Saturday, just before the May 1 holidays, when he wore one of those tight little Coca-Cola shirts? Our department was washing windows that time. Spring cleaning, you know. And in the meantime he's dragging this huge log across the yard with Angulaty and Loosin. So Veronika, the draftswoman from Room 3, sees him and screeches at the top of her lungs, "Quick, come quick! Oh, I'm going to die!" Everyone comes running over—"What is it?"—and Veronika's hanging onto the wall for dear life, gasping, "Look at him, look quick, the wind's blown his hair straight up just like a hoopoe!"

All the women, old Vasyl Zakharych and Tolik from the supplies department (he was carrying the water pails for us, since our group had a shortage of men)—the whole gang just surged toward the window. And Alexandra Lexandrivna (she's retired, but according to her contract she can still pick up a little cash anywhere she wants part time for up to half a year; it's in one of their clauses), anyway, she jumps up, trips over the drafting table (and, by the way, she's not supposed to eat anything fried or hard to digest), knocks out her kneecap on one of the sharp edges, flips over, and then the wardrobe falls on top of her. We had to call an ambulance.

"So how about it, Vereshchak, what do you think of our director now? Would you marry a guy like that?"

"I could be his lover and not get married," Zoyka answers, but is suddenly embarrassed by how far she's gone and covers her face with her hands, later to part them just wide enough around her lips to mouth an indictment of her friends: You have corrupted me as a woman!

Delighted laughter resounds through the room.

"Zoy, hey Zoy! What if you had to travel with him to Germany in a compartment for two?"

"He's not my type!"

"Oh, so the director is a 'type'?"

"I didn't say that!"

"Oh yes you did! We all heard you! You're in for it now! You can forget about your apartment, because he won't be signing any papers for you!"

"What do you mean? They promised!" Zoyka can barely hold back her tears.

"Oh, don't worry," the more experienced women console her. "We're only joking. As friends. Just to warn you about talking too much."

"All I want is one teeny-weeny room . . ."

"You'll get it. It's inevitable."

"What if they cheat me out of it?"

"You'll go see the director. I translated for you once, you'll say to him. Remember?"

"What if he says no?"

"Go to the minister. I once brought you papers from the conference, tell him. Don't you recall?"

"That was the deputy minister!"

"That's even better!"

"He's not going to remember!"

"Then you'll have to insist!"

"How?"

"Wait around in his reception room day and night."

"They'll throw me out."

Well, if you don't want them to throw you out this is what you do. When you walk in, thrust yourself into the center of the room right away. The main thing is to get your head in, your body can always follow later. Get in there, fall down, start crying, open his eyes to the truth. Here you are in your meetings all the time, tell him, and you don't even know how we live. You're being deceived! They're telling you one thing and doing another! Take our dorm, for instance. Valentyna makes a deal with the commandant. The commandant lets her bring anyone she likes into the room, I'm not going to mention who, I'm not a snitch, you know, you tell him, all the more since some of them are married. She leaves her key in the door from the inside, and I can't get in until they've satisfied all their urges, I have to freeze my ass off outside. Help me! Or take another example: The toilet bowl has cracked open. All that's left is a gaping hole and two narrow strips for my feet. And yesterday the pitcher I used for flushing purposes fell and broke.

"I'd be too embarrassed."

"Then keep suffering!"

"That's easy for you to say!"

"You head right over to see Toma," they tell her, "and get

all the details. Who. When. Where. Which building. What kind of documents you need. What references. And in the meantime, start quietly putting together a Komsomol recommendation, a history of employment with salary scale, present job description, residence record, an application, transcripts, diploma, medical certificate, psychological testing results, and summary notes. Don't write it down now! First go find out what's going on. You can celebrate later. Because you know what sorts of things can happen . . . "

"What?"

"You name it."

"Like what?"

Like, for example, a boy fell in love with a girl. And she fell in love with him. Both of their living situations were horrendous. He was in a dorm. She didn't have a residence permit. Or it was the other way around? Doesn't matter. Where are they supposed to meet? Just before the wedding he says, let's try the theater. Let's go, she says. So they go. But there are no tickets. Let's try the movies! They rush over. But the show has already started. Well, what are they to do now? It was February then. Anyway, they end up finding some garage. They tiptoe in. Turn on the car engine. Because the owner was a real nerd and forgot to lock the garage door. And that boy worked as a driver and had this special key that was good for all cars. Let's do it, he says to his fiancée, our wedding's coming up anyway. She says okay. And the engine and heater are going full blast . . . They found them dead in the morning. The whole collective was out at the funeral, they were dressed in white.

And it's not only the young ones! I just heard about a man who got together with the cashier from the grocery store. So they go to the garage. It was snowing then. They turned on the heater and, of course, died of carbon monoxide poisoning. When his wife saw him the next morning in that position, so to speak, she said: I'm not taking him. Bury him yourselves.

"Why are you telling me all this?" Zoyka Vereshchak is getting upset. "I'm not getting married, I'm getting an apartment!"

"It's hard to say what's more important," they tell her, "getting married or getting an apartment."

"If only nobody hexes me," Zoyka grabs her head in her hands.

"Run, talk to Toma," the women persist.

She jumps up to do just that, but the ring of the telephone stops her at the door. Her aunt wants her to buy a roll during lunch break. Not a French stick, but one of those six-kopeck rolls. And God forbid, not those city breads! Just a stick. If it's fresh.

"And if there aren't any, what should I get then?" Zoyka Vereshchak asks.

"Yes! A fresh one!" shouts the aunt. She's been a little deaf since the war.

Finally Zoyka is free to go, thanks everybody for their advice, and runs off for a heart-to-heart with the well-connected Toma.

A minute before the break Marusyk drops in from Software Programming. Marusyk has spent most of his conscious life writing his dissertation. He wants Vitya Maliatko to translate an article for him from an American journal.

"He stepped out," they tell him.

"When will he be back?"

"After two. But he's on another job now. An important assignment from the director's office. Ministerial level. Foreign-currency publication."

With these words the women rise and set course for lunch.

Her dream is to get through as many of the Liahushenko papers as possible while no one is breathing down her neck and then to make another attempt at escape.

"Screw the thermos, who cares if it broke, even if it were 'Made in China' a hundred times over," she whispers, dialing her home number again and again. The line is busy. It would be one thing if that's Volodya calling work to explain why he's still at home. But what if at this very moment he's dialing for an ambulance?

"I knew it," Antonina Pavlivna gives a start, "the dream was a warning!" Oh, if only she could stop time, turn it around, and send it back to the moment before disaster struck. Then run with all her might, pick up enough speed, and jump right over it. Can it really be that hard? Honestly, my Lord, please! Whom would it hurt?! If she could do that she'd be willing to . . . Well, anything at all! . . .

Trolley No. 8 rattles by outside the window. And they've just dropped off the apples around the corner, judging by the size of the crowd. Three paces beyond, a raven wards off two pigeons, not letting them get at a yellowish ham bone, which he expertly rolls ever further from the garage dogs. If she makes her move now, while the front door is unchecked, runs outside, and then sneaks through the hole in the garage fence to the avenue and flags down a cab right away, there's still a chance she can catch them at home.

She removes her hands from her face, massages her temples, and recalls how the day before yesterday Volodya tried to fasten Andriy's satchel strap with wire and almost cut his finger off.

"Aren't you ashamed of yourself?" she had said to Andriy as she bandaged Volodya's hand. "Your father almost became an invalid because of your sloppiness. I carried around my first schoolbag for seven years. Tell me truthfully, are you ashamed of yourself or not?"

"I'm ashamed," Andriy answers.

"Then why don't you say anything?" Antonina Pavlivna demands of her son.

"I'm looking at the lock," Andriy says.

"Which lock?" asks Volodya.

"The lock on the schoolbag," says Andriy.

"And what do you see there?"

"It's very transparent," Andriy says. "You can see three Andriys at the same time. And they're all looking at me, also an Andriy. And who really knows which of them is the real me?"

Antonina Pavlivna tries to get through to them one more time, once again to no avail.

"I'm dropping everything as is right now!" she assures herself. "What's more important to me, anyway?! I'll leave a note. Or I'll call from home. Because once the lunch hour is over I'll never get out!"

She grabs her kerchief, jumps into her coat in a flash, and is ready to leave. But she still needs to jot down a quick explanation. Antonina Pavlivna rummages through papers, swings open the cupboard door to the desk, searches for something on which to leave a few parting words. A cup and spoon, two biscuits wrapped in cellophane, a small skein of wool, a half-knitted child's sock, and a fat epic novel stare up at her with disapproval from the three veteran drawers. The novel is monstrous and clearly leads the pack. It draws Antonina Pavlivna toward itself like a magnet, paralyzes her, forces her to open it, and read about Vasyl.

And thus Vasyl, she reads, walks into the house, lights an unhappy cigarette (his thirty-fourth that evening) made of tobacco as tough as old man Yevmen, may God rest his soul. And no matter how many times Vasyl has promised himself he'll quit (oh curse this nasty habit!) and chided himself for his weak will, yet during the party cell meeting he succumbs, pours the old man's weed onto a yellow scrap of the district paper, rolls it, and singeing the fingers that have worked dawn to dusk since childhood, for generations, from time immemorial, he strikes a stealthy match in a dimly lit corner of the room. Somewhere deep inside him stirs a staunch unshakable revulsion to the critical musings of the director. But, having rejected this subjective factor, he cannot, as a veteran of the storming of Berlin and as lecturer in biology, chemistry, physics, astronomy, industrial arts, and phys ed, help but agree—our director Trokhym Pylypovych is right on the mark! It is this deeply ingrained sense of justice, this principled stand on the issues, that has earned our director such deep respect from the staff of Lenin Junior High.

Pungent smoke envelops Vasyl. The bitter, caustic, stinging, yet absolutely just words thrown at the harvest labor front under his command were countless. Of course, he could have pointed to a long list of weighty reasons to explain the productivity lag, but a nagging doubt gnaws at him, prevents him from resting on his laurels. Am I really as innocent as all that? In each and every way? What if I really thought about it? Scrutinized every motive? And what about yesterday, in the beet field, with that new German teacher fresh from college, when I distributed duties between grades 4A and 5B? Whose stern cry prevented her Pioneers from introducing a new extraction method? Whose fault was it that we fell short of the goal? The heart of the secondary school toiler pounds heavily. Blood, thicker than water, pumps through the arteries of his smoldering battered soul. How to overcome the shame of individual shortcomings? How to improve the ratings and get into first place yourself for a change?

What If Volodya Is Not Trying to Get Through to Emergency, But to That Lascivious Woman Ilona from the Department Down the Hall? A Horrible Thought Strikes Antonina Pavlivna

IT'S FINE AND DANDY THAT HE CAME OUT AND CONFESSED on his own that time. It happened in May, he said, somewhere between the lilacs and acacia trees. The central office had announced that their turn had finally come to round up the quota for the upcoming elections in the microdistrict. Two departments go out to enumerate the territory assigned to their institute. They go from apartment to apartment, compiling a list of eligible voters. Research engineer Ilona walks beside him, step in step, throughout. After completing their rounds they end up, in some way unbeknownst to themselves, on a very wide bench at the edge of the park. Darkness falls. He skips over the other details and confesses only that he had his hands on Ilona's breasts.

Antonina Pavlivna feels nauseous and empty all over again. How could he? And the main thing is—why? It's better not to know. Who asked him to tell her anyway? And what is she supposed to do with this knowledge now? Maybe things went a lot farther than he admits? He said that was the only time. In May. Just before the elections. And how is she to act now? Pretend that nothing has happened? He'll just do it again. An accident will turn into a bad habit and a bad habit into a sport. Push him away? He won't come back. Try to restrain him? He'll want to do it even more. That whore! He was probably taking her home from the election office. She probably dragged him into some darkened doorway, started talking about art, got close to him that way, and sent him into heat. Told him a whole bunch of lies about how her husband is a lousy lover and immediately divulged who was the first man to take her to bed. And, of course, all a bitch like that would need is a few strokes to start clawing, squeezing, slithering, moaning, shrieking, going into convulsions, so that finally, in victorious exhaustion, she could throw herself on the chest of a married man. Once. A second time. And then again. And the whole time biting Volodya's ear and telling him that nobody, but nobody, can do it the way he can.

But maybe none of that really happened? Well, so he touched someone else's breasts one tiny time, so what! It's a crime, but not a big one. Other guys do far worse! And he did confess on his own . . . Because he's a man of principle.

When he started on the new job the personnel officer said to him, "That beard could come off."

"Whose beard?" asks Volodya.

"Yours," says the officer.

"What about yours?" Volodya asks.

"Hmm?" says the officer. "I'm clean shaven. And, by all appearances, you're not. And around here, that almost comes under the national security guidelines."

After that he kept dragging his feet on the permanent placement paperwork, but Volodya didn't give in. It's not like he has one of those shaggy beards the size of a shovel. On the contrary, his is very neat, trimmed close to the face, he just needs to shave around the cheekbones a wee bit occasionally, and once a month I even it out for him and snip off the more unruly hairs.

Once Andriy asked him, "Why do you snip the hairs inside your nose? Don't you know how important they are? I read in a magazine that without those hairs the human race would have died off ages ago from sucking in all that dust and germs! It's a natural barrier. There's a Malagasian saying . . . "

"Malanesian?" Volodya queries.

"Malagasian!" Andriy insists.

"Where's that?"

"On the island of Madagascar. Right here!"

We have a map of the world in our kitchen. When Andriyko was six years old he could already name all the capitals of the world.

"I noticed," he said, "that Paraguay has a lot of cities starting with the letter Fortín. There's Fortín-Luis, Fortín-Coronel, Fortín-Hernandarias. How would you explain something like that?"

Volodya Is Very Talented, Too

NOT ONLY TECHNICALLY, BUT ALSO IN TERMS OF ART. HE once saw someone wearing mother-of-pearl jewelry, so he bought himself a workbench, collected a whole bag of shells. Get some holes in your ears, he said, I'm going to make you earrings. And he's not about to make the kind that everybody else wears, he's got something abstract on his mind, but for now he's keeping it a secret. Last weekend he ground up almost all his shells, there was smoke and dust all over the kitchen, but nothing came of it. The material is so brittle! The minute something begins to take shape it cracks. And Andriy's getting in the way all the time. I keep trying to distract him with the book *I Want to Know Everything* (ages 8 to 12) to get him away from that dust! And there's Volodya wanting to master the medium, going through hell, even though I did tie some gauze around his nose and mouth.

"Dad!" Andriy shouts from his room. "Do you know why we need hydrogen?"

"No, I don't."

"Should I tell you?"

"Please."

"For refrigerators. And also it can be used to make liquid oxygen, and then . . . Are you listening?"

"I'm listening. And then what?"

"What did I say last?"

"You said 'and then.'"

"Well?"

"Well, what?"

"What happens then?"

"How am I supposed to know?"

"Think!"

"I give up."

"No, you can't give up. You have to think about it. Give it three tries."

"I give up. Who does a pest like you take after, I wonder."

"I guess you don't really want to know."

"I do!"

"Are you sure?"

"Of course."

"Cross your heart!"

"I'm crossing it, I'm crossing it! Just stop pestering me!"

"And then the age-old dream of mankind can become a reality: a hydrogen engine!"

"Hurrah, I got it!" shouts Volodya, pulls me over to the workbench, and shows me an almost-ready earring of ambiguous shape about half the size of my ear.

"What does it remind you of?" he asks.

"It's hard for me to say right away," I tell him.

"Try."

"I can't."

"Then guess."

"I give up."

"No, think about it."

"Leave me alone!"

"What's going on here? I'm grinding my fingers to a pulp for her, and she doesn't even care."

"All right," I say, "what do you want me to do?"

"Guess what it reminds you of."

"Let me think."

"Does it remind you of Don Juan?"

"Uh . . . Not really."

"Why not? Take a closer look! It turned out exactly as conceived. Here you have the curls coming down to the shoulder, here's the distinctive profile . . . "

"Why did you decide to do Don Juan?"

"Here's half the mustache. The second half's going right here. Let me just . . . "

Volodya takes the graver (that's a kind of cutting instrument made of very strong steel), wants to chisel in the final groove, but the shell snaps into bits and crumbles to the floor. Volodya overturns the workbench, all the tools and shells gathered in the riverbed go flying, he tramples them, grinds them into the floor, and then stands on the balcony for half an hour without a hat.

He doesn't like going to the doctor. Pills, syrups, inhalations—doesn't believe in any of that. The body got into this mess, he says, it can get out on its own, I'm not going to meddle. He doesn't eat sour cream or eggplant salad, won't touch cake. But he can sure put away that fish! On the other hand, you can't really call him a fussy eater. If he doesn't like something, he simply makes himself a cup of tea with sugar and goes off to work hungry.

They have a very close-knit team at work. Whether it's mushroom picking, negotiating potatoes from a collective farm, moving furniture from one apartment to another for a colleague—they do everything as a group. Friday nights they go to the bathhouse for a good steam, and then it's over to someone's place for dinner. Either Arkady's, or Smyk's, or the Kucheruks', or our place. Volodya buys moonshine only from an old boy he knows in the village and filters it through charcoal one more time just to make sure.

But, to be perfectly honest, his friends don't completely satisfy him, because he works on his spiritual development as well. Last summer he got a Bible through someone he went to school with and read the entire New Testament and part of the Old.

This classmate of his stayed with us at my parents' dacha

for almost a week, and I took a dislike to him immediately. It's not that I begrudge him all that food, or that the vegetable plot has to be weeded, or that when they turn on the taps you have to drop everything and run to water the trees and the garden. Meanwhile, he's sitting in the kitchen, smoking, swilling that narcotic tea, and arguing with Volodya. First he doesn't like this film because there's not enough Grace there for him, then he doesn't like that book because it's full of half-truths, which are a lot worse than lies . . .

"And who the hell is going to let you tell the truth?" Volodya says to him. "Who would publish you in this country? Who'd ever hear about you?"

"Questions like that," responds the other fellow, "have no relevance to absolute reality, in other words, to the essence of existence and of being."

He likes to get philosophical about everything. No matter what Volodya says to him, he has to contradict it.

"What do you mean 'as an intelligent person'? Are you talking about Christ? About his deeds? Way to go, man! Did you think that one up all by yourself?"

Volodya thrashes about, wants to explain exactly what he had in mind, but his classmate only waves his arms dismissively (his hair, by the way, is longer than mine, and you'd think he could wash it once in a while!). "Have you ever studied the Holy Scriptures?" he asks Volodya, and there's nothing but contempt in his voice, and such arrogance! And he keeps urging him to recall the parable of this and the parable of that, or some kind of antediluvian proverb, or something from Mandelstam's poetry. How is Volodya supposed to know all that? Where could he have learned it?

"Who do you know of the Silver Age philosophers?" he asks. "Have you read Father Sergei Bulgakov, not Mikhail the writer but Sergei the reverend," he says, "about the immanent wisdom of all creation? You haven't? Well then, man! . . . What about Leontyev? What about Gershezon,

Frank, or Rozanov? Or *The Pillar of Veritas?* Then what have we got to talk about? You do a little reading, and then we can get into a discussion."

Volodya can only stare back helplessly, angry at himself for knowing so little. Under the tutelage of this nitwit, he compiles lists of books that he needs to study as basic reading: Plato, Plotinus, St. Augustine, Böhme—try rounding up this stuff! It doesn't help that my best friend has had borrowing privileges at the History Library for years.

Why are you listening to this bum? I ask Volodya. Look at him and look at you! A research engineer, a specialist in the area of instrument development, and a security guard at the boat rental office! And don't take any books from him, you hear me? No photocopies, nothing published abroad! And no prerevolutionary literature either, I'm begging you! We all know, I tell him, what kind of country we live in, what kind of people are in charge here. All the millions that they've murdered! They can do whatever they want with us! They'll strangle us with their bare hands. Don't worry, they'll find lots of volunteers for the job. And nobody, not your buddies, not our families, will be able to save us. They'll sit and keep quiet the way we sit and keep quiet. And this classmate of yours, where's he getting all these books from? What if he's working for them? Exposing fools like you?!

Vitya Maliatko Thinks that Everyone Has Gone to Lunch,
Kicks Open the Door to the Room, and Almost Falls Down

"WHAT THE FU . . . ?" HE MUTTERS IN SURPRISE.
Antonina throws her whole body against the Liahu-shenko papers as though they were her husband's illicit books and Vitya Maliatko, in a gray uniform and at the head of a goon squad, has just crashed through the door to do a search.

But in reality Vitya has turned up so early because he was not able to break off with NIIAA and instantly become a free artist. Although he was making moves in that direction. He honestly ran out to the lobby, but at that moment the figures of the assistant director and scoresheet girl loomed in his path, flipping through some kind of lists. Vitya chickened out and made it look like he was studying the banner that hangs over the entrance and exhorts institute personnel to give their all in fulfilling the plan.

"Enter, comrade," red letters on a white backdrop beckon menacingly. "You have stepped onto these astonishingly beautiful premises, a gift to you from the state. Do not forget that, in addition to this building, the Fatherland has bestowed on you everything else: secondary or a higher education at will, good habits, quick reflexes, acquired in the course of stiff competition, and the clarion call of a radiant common future. Cherish them as you cherish communal property and individual conscience. Because millions of honest workers in your field stand with you, shoulder to shoulder, on the bulwarks of progress, faithfully bringing together the seeds of their knowledge and the fruits of their labor. Use wisely every one of the 492 minutes in the course of your working day! Remember, every such minute is costing the Fatherland 666 rubles!"

The cozy couple cuts off the exit until lunchtime rolls around, and thus Vitya only gets out to the street on the crest of a wave of starving NIIAA workers. The first thing he does is look for a pay phone, for he wants to ask a certain young lady if she regrets that yesterday she instructed him so categorically to leave her in peace. The pay phone swallows two coins. Vitya runs to the avenue where two telephone booths stand on the corner. But the first hasn't worked from the moment of installation and in the other one (this part he didn't know) someone had ripped out the receiver. In the end he finds an undamaged telephone, dials the number with a trembling finger, and hears a familiar voice.

"Ahoy!" He tries his utmost to sound indifferent. "Do you recognize my divine baritone?"

The baritone is recognized

"Do you regret the events of yesterday?"

She does not.

"And tonight's concert?"

"Count me out."

"Good enough, then."

"Great."

Vitya Maliatko hangs up, pulls out two tickets, tears them into tiny pieces over the trash can, and in his pocket notebook crosses out the name of a once very close friend as well as her telephone number.

That's the end of that! Time to turn over a new page. But why isn't he rushing home, where a sketchbook and an assortment of paints await him? Or to the great outdoors, where the spirit can break free and create? Could he have really had a change of heart? By no means. But first, rather than be a hothead (and he knows he has a tendency to do this), it would be worthwhile to establish once and for all, for himself at least, the scope of his talent. Because desire on its own is not enough to achieve success. Or glory, for that matter.

The Arrival of Ophelia Feliksivna and Svitlana Zhuravlynchenko Signals that the Lunch Break Is Over

"TODAY THE CAFETERIA HAD LOVELY PORK CHOPS À LA Trans-Siberian Express," Svitlana Zhuravlynchenko announces. "But I had some goulash instead. It wasn't bad."

Ophelia Feliksivna walked all the way over to the deli for lunch and was also satisfied with her steamed cutlets served with sour cream and cottage cheese. For dessert she had compote.

The women get back to their conversation, begun in the elevator, about last night's concert on TV.

"So what did you think of that Neliadina? The bag's over fifty, and the way she was hopping around . . . "

"In a negligee, yet."

"Shaking her ass all over the stage, if you'll pardon me for saying so."

"Some choice for the National Arts Medal! And on Policemen's Day! It's a travesty!"

"Before, like about twenty-five years ago, she didn't move too badly. Mind you, her vocal skills were never much . . . "

"There's a time and a place for everything."

Vitya Maliatko peers into his little black book. Almost every page has a thickly crossed out woman's name.

"If at least the creativity end of it would come through!" He appeals to God-knows-whom for God-knows-what. "It's either lucky at love or lucky at art!"

"So who did you say she's having an affair with now?" Svitlana Zhuravlynchenko wants to know.

"Valery Blokotov!"

"That's impossible! Everybody knows that Valery Blokotov's wife . . . "

"So?!"

"And what about the fact that the Politburo made it voluntarily compulsory for figure skaters of a certain level to marry their current skating partners?"

"That's impossible!"

"Impossible or not, it's true! You know who told me?"

"I don't care who told you! You think about it yourself for a moment." Ophelia Feliksivna demonstrates a proper measure of sound judgment. "Is the Politburo going to waste its time discussing the goings-on between Larysa Toughka and Oleh Griazev? As if they don't have a State Sports Committee for that!"

"So who, then," Svitlana Zhuravlynchenko insists on an answer, "who's Neliadina's lover now?"

"The one who loves Neliadina now," Vitya Maliatko pushes his way into other people's conversation, "is the food taster at the Lycra-wear factory!"

The women burst out laughing.

"And what do you know about all this?" Ophelia Feliksivna's shoulders stiffen. She is convinced that Vitya Maliatko is not so much making fun of Neliadina, or even of Svitlana, as he is of her.

"Tamara Zakharivna Lupova was asking," she tries to frighten Vitya, "how the director's book is coming along."

"For Neliadina! On guard!" Vitya Maliatko jumps up, pushes the chair out of the way, and spins through the air in such a way as to line himself up not with the window but with Ophelia Feliksivna. Another second, and some uncontrollable force propels him directly toward a surprised and somewhat excited woman so that he can either kiss her, bark into her ear, or bite her finger. Because how else can he pour out the pain of a broken heart and compensate for the absence of creative achievement?

"What am I doing, am I nuts?" he asks himself. "It would be so nice if the door opened this minute and Lupova walked in with Woodnov, saying, relax, we know that you're one our gifted boys. Tomorrow nature will send you water, frost, and patterns on the window that will make today's designs (believe us!) bitterly regret that they did not turn themselves over to you, that they were in such a hurry to vanish, that they couldn't be bothered to get themselves immortalized on paper and so step directly into eternity. Because you are an artist of the kind that does not come along very often. But before the world finds out about this, why don't you, Vitya, old chum, do us one small favor: Pop over to the ministry and drop off this package. And when you have completed this assignment, don't bother coming back, fly off in all four directions!"

But nobody hastens to Vitya Maliatko's rescue. Ophelia Feliksivna is right in front of him, you can see her even without a horoscope. A Leo, her hair a thick luxuriant mane, the smile of a capricious girl, an amber pendant purchased at a Baltic resort. Will he really have to, for the sake of purity of the genre, collide into this innocent unmarried woman, hard enough to be taken off to prison?

He hears no answer.

Ophelia Feliksivna can't believe how she could have gotten herself into this preposterous position. It's ludicrous! Madness! Everywhere! In everything! No, no, she's got to get out of this country! Right away!

She arms herself with a sharp and agile metal ruler. The other women prepare identical smiles in anticipation of laughter. It seems as though Vitya Maliatko is doomed, that either Ophelia Feliksivna, untempered as she is by communal street fights, will fly headfirst into the wall, or he will stab himself on her keen-edged centimeters. In any case, at any moment blood will gush in all directions, and from that horror someone is bound to faint.

But They Are Saved from Prison and Grievous Injury by a Tear-Stained Zoyka Vereshchak, Who Suddenly Pops Up in the Doorway

SHE LOOKS NO DIFFERENT THAN ALWAYS—HER HAIR PULLED back in a simple bun; her dress carries no more than the usual amount of lint and hairs; her two side teeth, the absence of which becomes apparent only when she smiles, are still missing as they were an hour ago. And the faint odor coming from her mouth has also not dissipated. But the uplifted mood of the morning is gone. Her body exudes outrage, intensified lachrymal secretion, and pangs of bittersweet anguish.

"Well?" her sympathetic colleagues approach. From up close they see that one of the buttons of her brand-new dress has been sewn on with much lighter thread.

"Well? Tell us everything, exactly as it happened. Don't leave us in suspense this way!"

Zoyka Vereshchak throws herself on the desk and for some time sobs, choking on her grief. The others try to calm her down and find out in the process that bigmouth Toma got it all screwed up. What they discussed at the trade union meeting last night was not the distribution of apartments, but rather the construction of a new prefab high-rise for young specialists. At this point it's not clear yet precisely where it will shoot up, who will be the future contractor, or when and who will live there. The idea came from the Komsomol youth of NIIAA, NIITS, and TSNIPIZU, but rumor has it that HIDROFUKS wants to jump in on this as well. That would be a disaster, because HIDROFUKS has more youth than the first three institutes put together.

"So what's wrong with that," Zoyka's girlfriends console her, "aren't you one of our young specialists? On the postgraduate distribution of professional cadres quota? Aren't you in the Komsomol?"

"It's too la-ate!" the Komsomol girl confesses. "As of September my membership expired for reasons of age. And you're only considered a junior specialist for the first three years! And this is already year five! And besides, they're all married, with children! They'll get in first! And in the meantime, my toilet in the dorm is broken again, and spotted rats are squeezing in through the hole . . . "

"What a nightmare! When? Where? How? All the way up to the fourth floor? Why haven't you said anything?"

"Because we don't have them yet. But they can survive a nuclear holocaust, you know, I read it in a book (them and the spiders), and they can scratch their way to the top of a television tower. Have you seen their claws?! I saw one out in back of the grocery store the other week, and I thought I would die right then and there. But I changed my mind, because if I fell down it would have crawled over and ripped a piece of my face off!"

"Oh my God!"

"Why didn't you ask them to put your name down?"

"For what?"

"On the list."

"What list?"

"Any list."

"Where is it?"

"With the administration. That's the way it works, always, no matter what they're planning to do, they first and foremost draw up a secret list."

"So how do I get in there?"

"You have to pull strings."

"That's easy for you to say . . . "

"And you must never give up! . . . "

"You can afford to preach! You've got somewhere to live!"

"You listen to us. Hope is the most important thing."

"What hope? There's nothing but ashes left in my soul."

You Can't Get Through Life Without Ashes, They Tell Her,
But You Need Hope, Too

DO YOU KNOW WHAT HAPPENED TO A FRIEND OF MINE WHO lost all hope because of love and was ready to go out the window? She took a nice long bath for the last time, dried herself off well, ran across the room as fast as she could, and jumped, but she missed the pavement and landed instead on a luxuriant willow tree all covered in snow. The willow cushioned the woman's fall and then, as if it were a skating rink, deposited her out on the road. And it just so happened that an ambulance was driving by. The woman related absolutely everything to the surprised paramedics, and they told her not to be so stupid after this and not to take her young life and such an exceptional figure so lightly on account of some wretched lover. But then suddenly this huge Belarus tractor-trailer crashes into the ambulance. The woman sustains serious injuries with broken bones and amputations while the ambulance driver and paramedics get off with minor scratches. And all because she didn't have hope!

"Oh, honestly! What's all this talk of hope?!" Zoyka continues to swallow her tears. "What good is hope?"

Ah, you just listen, they tell her. There is another woman who also fell in love and on account of these feelings decided to drown herself. But all the same she didn't lose hope. So she waited until work was over, got on a streetcar, and she's riding around, trying to decide where the best place is to jump into the swirling vortex. As she winds her way on this public transit vehicle in the direction of the nearest river, sighing bitterly, it occurs to her that in our country you can get into a lot of trouble for pulling a stunt like this. No sooner does she think that than a plainclothes man comes up to her and says, come with me. Oh no, the woman begins to cry, I won't do it again, let me go! But she doesn't lose hope, you see. All right, the man says, then give me the name and address of your place of work and the number and address of your passport. She gave everything to him as he asked. You'll come tomorrow to such and such a place. All right. I will. The woman rides on. But suddenly she gets so hungry that she has to get off and go into a dining hall. She gets in line, gets her soup, her hot meal, some compote, wipes her spoon with a napkin. And she's just about to take the first bite when she notices the cooks bringing out a full kettle of cheese dumplings. Oh, they'll be gone by the time I get there, they'll be gone! But she doesn't lose hope. She grabs her portion, pays for it, returns to her seat, and can't believe her eyes! There's a black man sitting in her place, slurping the bowl of borscht that she paid for! She begins to tremble and shake all over (you know how nerves can be!), but still she sits down beside him and glares with the appropriate amount of venom. The black man acts like butter wouldn't melt in his mouth. Finishes the soup, starts into the hot meal, polishes that off, then wraps his grayish-pink fingers around the compote. He swallows it in a few careful, dignified gulps, wipes his lips with a clean handkerchief, gets up, and leaves. Here the woman can't take it anymore. She lets out a terrible cry, jumps on top of that table with her boots, and hurls her plate of cheese dumplings at the chandelier. When suddenly she notices her tray on the neighboring table, with her soup, hot meal, and compote standing there untouched . . .

"So what does all this have to do with me?" Zoyka still can't understand. "You know I don't like compote."

"Listen, Zoy!" Somebody gets an unexpectedly brilliant idea. "Can't you do something through your aunt?"

"What has my aunt got to do with this?!"

"You can apply pressure through her! You hinted at this yourself. Isn't she somebody . . . ? What's her biography, her title, her distinctions? Tell us."

Zoyka Vereshchak wipes her long-since-dry eyes with her small round fists, brushes a few flecks of dandruff from her shoulders, and piles her dictionary, journal, notebook, sheet of writing paper, crumpled handkerchief, and apple core into a rather crooked yet still quite recognizable pyramid.

"My aunt," she says solemnly, "is a decorated Member of the Order, it's only the Order of Labor, mind you, and for the war all she got was a medal, but all the same our district newspaper wrote about her twice, once with her picture. She's retired now with honor on a well-deserved pension, yet she doesn't shy away from the schoolchildren, attends meetings, and shares her experience with younger colleagues. But mostly she shares her memories of her father, the legendary revolutionary leader, guerrilla fighter, and hero of heavy industry, who raised the banner for the first collective farm in our parts and so met his untimely death—Pervomay Ivanovych Vereshchak."

You've Read Flaming Smoke *by Vaillis and Krutykh?*

SHALL I TELL YOU? YES OR NO? AT LEAST BRIEFLY? IF YOU insist. Well then . . . He was one of those people, let me say to you first of all, rarely to be found in one's lifetime, a man of optimistically tragic fate . . . What? . . . No. Or rather, well, how can I put it . . . It's a novel, but at the same time— it's the truth.

The authors found hundreds of witnesses, compiled, edited, and adapted the materials, and told everything exactly as it was. Because Pervomay (that was his name in the underground) Ivanovych, due to the damned czarist regime, never knew his father, a proletarian peasant of the most downtrodden category, without any land or cow. Nonetheless, Comrade Budonny himself loved him for his victoriousness—him and Burya the orderly, who was chopped up by the Whites back then. That's what the book says. Vaillis and also Krutykh reveal his great love for everything that is truly ours: the implacability of his convictions, his principled stand on raising the new generation, on the friendship of nations and hatred toward the enemy. There's this one episode in there . . . Just out of this world! . . . You're not listening! Who do you think I'm straining my vocal cords for? You think I need this? I knew that *Flaming Smoke* by heart by the time I was six years old. I even know all the features of his character. The perseverance, the love of life, the early steeling of will and body, the uncommon seriousness for a child so young, his grasping the significance of sacrificial heroism, the depth and breadth of his organizational abilities . . . So shall I continue? In general terms? Year by year? Or shall I get into the heroic deeds right away? Whatever's more interesting for you. I'll be very brief.

To make a long story short, as a young man Pervomay was a true friend, loving son, and gentle father. All the folks in the countryside noted his poetic nature, his sensitivity and directness. Especially when it came to Voulia, on their first date . . . You should see what happens after that! . . . But, one thing at a time! . . . Are you listening? Then why are you . . . Okay!

Anyway, just one glance, and he senses her spiritual needs right away. Her loneliness in implementing the ratified decisions, the conflict between the quivering tremor of her ideals and the drive to duty. You've probably figured it out already? No? You're kidding! Voulia is my aunt's mother! Later Bandit Butterfly's units . . . I understand. Well, you're the ones who asked me. I'll just give an outline. The most important moments.

As soon as he, Pervomay Vereshchak, found out about this, he matured immediately and gave an oath, and he realized that from now on the stress must be placed on discipline. He was joined by Pronko, Howdy, and Dovator. But not Bdzholkin—he only reaches the correct decision at the end. And so, as the hardcore backbone of the organization, he battles for the party line. And the saboteurs, on the contrary, with the help of the local passive masses, are resisting; they want to subvert the banner and gnaw and cut through the network lines. Sensing the imminent victory of the Cause, Pervomay Vereshchak utters the prophetic words in the clearing during a conversation with his daughter (That's my aunt! She had just started crawling then). Oh, if only he had known that the serpents were already lying in wait in the nettle with their shotguns. My heart begins to palpitate every time I read the part about his death! But don't you worry. That very night the district central command sent over a shock troop unit to neutralize all of them.

"So there you have it," Zoyka Vereshchak summarizes. "I can get the book from my aunt (his daughter, that is) if somebody wants to borrow it, as long as you return it fairly soon."

"Um, yeah . . . " the audience hems and haws, "we'll have to do that . . . Just as soon as I get a little caught up . . . There's so much work at home . . . I still haven't been able to get through my *World Literary Supplement . . .* "

In other words, there are no volunteers to drop everything and start reading *Flaming Smoke*.

Zoyka looks around. The women suddenly become interested in the Liahushenko report.

"I see!" says Zoyka. "When all illusions are shattered, and when feelings . . . or rather, faith . . . hope for the better . . . love . . . No! . . . It's all a sham . . . All lies and jest! How? For what? With no motivation, no incentives . . . Black indifference . . . "

The clattering phone interrupts her thoughts.

"Did you get it?" the aunt inquires of Zoyka Vereshchak.

"Get what?"

"What do you mean, what? The goose!"

"What goose?"

"Are you trying to be funny? I asked you yesterday, I begged you! You know it's hard for me to walk. At the corner there, not far from your work, the super's wife said— you had a lunch break, didn't you?—geese, grade B, two-sixty a kilo, half the gizzards out already. I gave you my last plastic bag yesterday, didn't I, cellulose, I washed it and hung it up to dry in the bathroom and I gave it to you. She doesn't need it, I told myself, but then I reconsidered, oh, I'll give it to her, what if she stumbles on something, like, for instance, I haven't had halvah in a while, and she runs around all over, not like me with my legs swelling, and I need vitamins, too, and protein. I've still got porridge, and pickles, and then what's-her-name calls that they've just thrown out some geese somewhere! Honestly! That head of yours is full of holes!"

"If you only knew . . . "

"I don't need to know anything! If I could just get a little respect from you . . . "

"How can you say that! As if I don't . . . I have to work. How can I . . . "

"How? How? How now, brown cow!" shouts the aunt and slams the receiver, because all this how-how has sent spasms up and down her body and a rash over her yellow skin.

"Why can't she just nap in peace?!" Zoyka Vereshchak addresses her co-workers. "Why does she always want something from me?!"

"Because you are her only support in life," venture the more generous in spirit.

"Maybe she's one of those domestic vampires?" the others tell Zoyka. "And she has to keep you by her side as a source of blood?"

"What's that?" Zoyka forgets to shut her mouth in fright and a stray tear rolls inside.

"Your aunt," those who know explain, "probably has a need to control you all the time, because she has a weakened energy-supply mechanism. Have you ever noticed that in her?"

"I don't know."

"And after being in contact with her have you ever felt a kind of sharp, even a little dull, inexplicable sadness? A weakness? Or a fear of loneliness?"

"Well, normally, I . . . "

"Then that's it!"

"What do I . . . "

There Was Once a Woman, They Explain to Her, Who Used to Suffer Terribly from the Evil Eye of a Close Friend

BUT SHE WAS UNAWARE OF THIS. SHE USED TO BE SICK A LOT and was always getting herself into one scrape after another. She went to a fortune-teller. The fortune-teller says: Well, well well. You'll have a birthday party soon, the last one to leave will be your tormentor, and she'll ask for money to get home. Don't give her anything.

The birthday came. They had a great time, ate a lot (she got this fantastic pork loin!), had a bit to drink, of course. It came time for the guests to leave. Only her best friend stays behind. Lend me some money for taxi fare, she says, because it's dark already and I'd like to get home soon. She's won't do it. I don't have that much, she says. Well then give me enough for the bus! I don't have it. At least give me a token. I'm all out. Whatever you've got, I'll take a used transfer, I don't care! I don't have a thing. Her best friend falls to the floor and begins to plead, begins to rip and tear the parquet out with her nails: Give me something, please, please! No matter what she tried, nothing worked. She had to leave empty-handed. But after that this woman, the one who used to be sick a lot, became happy and rosy-cheeked. And the witch got all dried out and pale, and turned a blackish-yellow color.

"You know," Zoyka confesses to her colleagues, "I really don't feel like living anymore."

"You have to!" they all start convincing her.

"What for?!"

"For your apartment, at the very least!"

"What apartment?!"

"Your future one!"

"Oh, right, they'll give me one just like that!"

"So the hell with them. But you have to fight!"

"How?" says Zoyka. "Teach me!"

"All right. Sit down and listen. The first thing you do is you run over to your aunt's this very day and say, well, here's the story, it's no secret for all concerned that I am an orphan. You are, you tell her, my most near and dear relative. Today it was a chicken that you needed . . . "

"A goose!" Zoyka Vereshchak corrects the error.

"That's even better! Today it was a goose you needed, but tomorrow there may not be anyone to pass you a glass of tap water. There's obviously only one solution here—you have to get me registered in this town. I invoke you, in the proud name of Vereshchak."

"All I want is one teeny corner of my own!" Zoyka explains. "Just one . . . "

"And then she can say," Zoyka's associates proceed to instruct her, "she can say this: Well, it's true what you say, I have no children of my own, move in and live with me, it'll be merrier for both of us. And just as soon as she agrees, you go that very day, or better yet, first thing the next morning, before she has a chance to change her mind, you run over to the ZHEK, grab ID Form No. 3, a statement from the dorm, and two applications. ZHEK is going to resist, because if your aunt dies and you're not registered there, ZHEK gets the apartment back. But what you do is target the specific person handling your case and shower her with an avalanche of chocolates, pantyhose, and perfume."

"I'm not asking for a lot." Zoyka wants to be completely honest. "If I could just get registered anywhere, anywhere at all!"

"And if your aunt," the lesson continues, "begins to babble, I got you registered, I thought you'd be scrubbing out my night potty every morning, and you're throwing parties with guitar music, you want to run me off the face of the earth, you whore, where are your ideals, then you tell her: You shut up right this very minute! And stop running around blabbermouthing to all the neighbors, because I'll send you away for treatment to the insane asylum for a year and transfer your savings account to my name. And should you chew your way through the barbed wire and escape from the nuthouse, then I'll put out an ad for an apartment trade, and all you'll get is a dank smelly corner of a communal flat, while I shall receive such a suite that, in the event of a closer acquaintanceship with a tall, shy, and wealthy doctoral candidate, we'll be able to pool our square meters and, as a result, take possession of a spacious two- . . . no! better yet, three-room apartment in the city center. Have you understood everything I just said or not?"

"I wouldn't be able to say that!"

"You'll learn. Come on, Vereshchak, get with it." Everyone is anxious to give Zoyka support. "Things don't just happen by themselves, you have to hustle! Here's a newspaper for you, take it, there are all kinds of ads in here for apartment trades. Study them, get an idea of what you need, find out what's available, they give you all the phone numbers, go ahead, call, take an interest. The sky's the limit! . . . "

"It's easy for them to give advice," Zoyka grumbles, "they're not the ones who'll have to do it, they're not the ones who'll be talking to my aunt. Let's assume, for the sake of argument, I say to her . . . "

The seven-foot-tall supervisor of technical personnel, Lyonia Spichek, and Lupova walk into the room. He holds in his hands a flowchart explaining the application of automated management systems to the entire field. Two departments worked on the model, Lyonia's people cut out and outfitted the base and did all the drawings. But before writing the names of departmental subdivisions into the empty rectangles and demonstrating the effect of the introduction of methods, it is necessary to have the editors check each and every word.

"Do us this favor, what are friends for?" Lupova orders Ophelia Feliksivna, to whom Lyonia Spichek was just showing his board. Ophelia Feliksivna points him in the direction of Svitlana Zhuravlynchenko and issues the appropriate command. By virtue of that same command, Svitlana is joined by Antonina Pavlivna.

Ophelia Feliksivna returns to the Liahushenko papers and undisguisedly, so that those above can see the extent to which she is overworked, shakes her head so caught up in the details of production.

But in reality she is asking herself the rhetorical question: How much longer can such absurdity go on?

And She Answers: A Hundred Years, For All I Care, But Without Me!

IN HER LAST LETTER KARINA WROTE (YOU CAN WAIT UNTIL doomsday before you get a letter from Ella!) that the summer whizzed by scarcely without notice, but she did manage to get a tan, although she didn't go on vacation, but took math, health, cooking, and driving in summer school. The program was "accellorated," every day they did a "unut," and then they had a "tast," which went into the overall "graid."

Rather than the usual vacation at the seashore somewhere in Crimea or the Caucasus, she worked seven hours a day, five days a week, in cash at the shoe store. She got more tired out this month than in all her previous years of school back in the USSR. But, she now has a check for four hundred dollars! Not bad, eh? And besides, she writes, they've introduced a new system for us: if you sell two pairs to one customer, you get a dollar "ekstra," three pairs—three dollars, four pairs—six, five pairs—ten. Did you understand how this works? If not, I can explain it in more detail.

For two—one, for the third—two, for the fourth—three, and for the fifth—four, in other words, all together, for five pairs, you have ten dollars "ekstra." It sounds funny the first time you hear it, doesn't it?—one dollar, two, then three— but, if you look closely and concentrate a little, a month later you have more than sixty.

I now have a goal—choose anyone concretely and get them to buy as many pairs of shoes as possible. And before? We "sailspersons" *didn't want to* strain ourselves with various questions, like "Can I help you?" (in English, of course). Not to mention things like "Would you like me to lace up your shoe?" What for? We got paid by the hour. It's more fun to spend the time talking to each other, don't you think? But these days everyone is jumping the clients one ahead of the other so they can make more of those "ekstra" dollars. The store makes a profit and we make a profit, and everybody's happy and everybody feels great. So that's how the capitalist West is rotting away! Did you understand everything?

Thanks to this system I have begun to master a very important concept, which is called: *you have to know how* to make money. It always starts with something small, with the first dollar. But it's already begun! And here you have the results—sixty dollars in one month! In other words, I can do it! Ah, it's so important—to know how to make money. Especially in a country like this! Where you have so many opportunities! I feel so sorry for all of you! And especially for those fifteen years I didn't spend out here.

I'm sending you nine photographs of me. I especially wore different clothes for each one and used our lockers as a backdrop, so that you could get an idea where every student in our school keeps his books and coat. As you can see, each locker has a lock with a code. And each of us has a personal key and has to remember his code. If it's your birthday, you decorate your locker with balloons and ribbons. It's convenient, pleasant, and looks nice, don't you agree?

"Don't be an idiot! Drop everything and get out here!" the letter teases from between the lines.

Ophelia recognizes the voice of Karina's mother—Ella. Their parents both came out of the same communal flat on Liebknecht-Luxemburg Street. But Felix became an ophthalmologist renowned throughout the city while Fima was appreciated for his jokes only by neighbors, relatives, and the staff of the typewriter repair shop. This was the cause of the unequal conditions for the blossoming and ripening of their daughters. While Ophelia was ruining her eyesight studying *Rudiments of Piano Technique* and committing to memory Latin sayings about lions that never chase mice, Ella fought with the guys on the street and absorbed some folkloric expressions of her own. She knew what you had to say when they harassed you to share your doughnut ("forty-one—food for one") and how to behave when the underage goyim called you a *zhydivka* (you're supposed to say "yids have smarter kids" and hurl rocks at their heads).

No matter where they would go, Ella was always at the center of attention. Unlike Ophelia, who got straight A's in school, and used to win in all the panel debates, and graduated from the Faculty of Philology with a Diploma of Red Distinction, and is still pining away without a man.

"First of all," Ophelia puts her in her place, "what is the meaning of this tone of voice?" (Actually, she understands that this is Ella's defense mechanism at work.) "And second, . . ."

"You listen up!" Ella puts on the heat. "I know life! This ain't one of your colloquiums or solfeggios. And most of all (believe you me!) *fortuna non penis.* So you get the fuck out of that shithole NIIAA of yours (Ella was always so vulgar and knew all the swearwords) and get your ass down to OVIR, exit visa section . . . "

"That's enough!" Ophelia Feliksivna has heard enough. "If you dare, just one more time . . . "

"Kiss my *tuchis!*" Ella waves her perfectly manicured nails in the air. "You want to live like a white person? Then listen to me!"

"I do not want to listen to you!" replies Ophelia Feliksivna.

"You're insane! Ophelia, you are insane!" Ella is shouting now. "This the deal of a lifetime, I guarantee you 100 percent!"

"There is no need to guarantee me anything," says Ophelia Feliksivna. "And as far as OVIR goes, I haven't the foggiest notion where this establishment can be found."

"I'll explain everything!"

"There happen to be," Ophelia Feliksivna raises her voice in a attempt to drown out her sonorous friend, "there happen to be certain rules, certain legally notarized documents, which note, among other things, the degree to which blood ties . . . "

"Oh, Ophelia, give me a break!"

"How can you even suggest this! Don't you know that after Papa and Mama passed away I have nobody left!" Ophelia Feliksivna's chin quivers. Sadness and sorrow well into her eyes like acid.

"What's the problem?!" Pragmatic Ella can't understand. "I'll find you a hundred and one relatives! Solomon Moiseyevich Bass. How is he not your relative? A lawyer. Elderly. Lives in Los Angeles. He can do anything. You need an Israeli invitation?"

"Ah, Ella!" pleads Ophelia Feliksivna. "Does everything have to be a joke to you?"

"That's a good one!" Ella says to her. "Who the hell's joking? Consider the invitation in your pocket. Drop your scribble, grab a cab . . . "

"You say this as if you don't know that I never take taxis!"

"Oh, well then. Beeg deel! Get on the trolleybus!"

"Ah, Ella, if only it were all so easy!"

"And I'm telling you: Get on the trolley, just not at Cosmonaut Square, because there's always a goddamned kahal there with everybody from the 8th and 69th jamming together. Get on at Urytsky Av, a stop sooner. Take a seat by the window . . . "

"Well, let's assume I do that," Ophelia Feliksivna gives in, "what happens if I'm too late there, too?"

"Ophelia!" Ella hisses from the other side of the cold Atlantic. "Stop fucking with my mind!"

This kind of brutality Ophelia Feliksivna cannot withstand. She rises, unnoticed, and with quiet, dignified, submissive steps makes her way to the bus stop.

Naturally, given the laws of turpitude, a mob of hunched, tense, and desperate persons accompany her in the wait. After a chaotic storming of the public transit vehicle, heated threats from the driver through the microphone, and a few false starts, the trolleybus finally departs. For a while they all ride silently. Everyone presses against his or her neighbor, breathing directly in each other's face. Vapors from alien

nostrils and mouths swarm with viruses and bacilli. If someone sneezes, droplets with mutations of dangerous diseases
are spewed over a three-meter radius. If someone coughs, it's
five meters. Sometimes it's the other way around.

"So what's happening with the Makharchuks?" someone
beside her asks.

"They're doing all right. What's supposed to happen?"

"And Marusia?"

"Marusia retired. Fifty-six rubles."

"That's not much."

"She had about as much seniority as a donkey's ass. Mind
you, she did get herself in as an checker at our plant about a
year ago."

"I see . . . And what about Nadka. Married yet?"

"Um-huh."

"And Kolia? Out of the cooler?"

"Yeah."

"Drinking?"

"Less."

Poor, miserable people! Ophelia Feliksivna is hemmed in
from all sides, scarcely breathing. Is it their fault that they've
never known a different life? It's hard to imagine that somewhere parallel to them exists a Raphael or Einstein, an
Eisenstein, Thomas Mann, Picasso, Pasternak, Modigliani,
Toulouse-Lautrec, or Renato Guttuso.

"Dog yours?" an anxious grandfatherly type asks his
neighbor.

"No. I'm doing a favor for . . . "

"Who?"

"Borya, from Number 16."

"Not the one that died?"

"No."

"Aha, that wasn't Borya. I got it mixed up. That was
Lyonia that died!"

"Did you get him immunized?" a not-very-young woman
butts into the conversation. "And are you aware that accord-

ing to the most recent regulations dogs are not allowed on public transit?"

"But he's in a bag!"

"All the more! It's because of people like you that we have a rabies epidemic raging in the city!"

"Maybe it's because of people like you!"

That's it! Here we go! predicts Ophelia Feliksivna and tries to push her way closer to the exit. And can it be any different in these conditions? Enclosed space everywhere and always breeds xenophobia. Just think of Sparta. The sooner I get to OVIR the better!

But in order to do this she must first get around two women, one of whom is pregnant. Because of their modest height they cannot reach the handrails and are forced, so as not to fall on the turns, to squat and lean into those around them.

"Careful!" cautions a fat man who has comfortably settled into a single seat and is now digging the dirt out from under his nails with a matchstick.

"Maybe you'd like to get up!" he is advised. "There's a pregnant woman here."

"How am I supposed to know she's pregnant?!" the old boy answers. "I can't see . . . "

"You should be ashamed!" they explain to him.

"Why?" He is genuinely surprised. "I have a right!"

How is it, Ophelia Feliksivna wonders, that these people, whom I generally find quite likable, can possess such a lack of consideration for their fellow beings? A lack of consideration that so easily turns to hatred. Hatred for whom? For themselves, primarily! I reject the mystical approach, sweetened by sugary romanticism. Everything must have a rational explanation.

"Ignorant boor!" the pregnant woman's friend denounces the fatso. "He's snarling back yet!"

"You little dipshit!" he responds. He snorts, offended, but gets up.

"Idiot! Alla! Here, sit down! Don't pay attention to the cretin!"

Maybe the explanation can be found in the geography? Ophelia Feliksivna searches for an answer. The plains mentality, unmitigated by either mountains or the sea? Centuries spent in slavery? Maybe if you threw other nations into our conditions—let's take those very same Americans—their rage would boil over even more violently. And maybe rather than perfecting the art of uncensored utterance they would have blown each other off the face of the earth years ago.

"Shut your trap!" the agitated fat fellow advises his lady opponent. "Barely out of diapers . . . snot driveling down your . . . "

"Moron, yourself! Piece of shit!"

"Take it easy, bitch, shooting off your mouth like that. In just a minute you'll be collecting your teeth all over this . . . "

"And I'll scratch all your eyes out!"

The real paradox in the situation here, Ophelia Feliksivna concludes to her own surprise (she is shielded from the epicenter of the quarrel by two teenagers, a woman and her daughter, and a man in a tall hat), lies in the fact that under such conditions—oppression, stagnation, persecution—the true intelligentsia, in the form of a chosen few, has everywhere and always nurtured and cherished the highest cultural values.

As if in evidence of this statement, Ophelia Feliksivna suddenly hears, in the midst of the fracas that is by now sucking passenger after passenger into its black belly, a quiet and reasoned conversation.

"So the grandfather of your grandfather is who?"

"My great-great-grandfather."

"And seven times seven gives you how much?"

"Forty-nine."

"And when does water turn to ice?"

"At zero degrees Celsius."

Ophelia Feliksivna leaves her warm familiar spot in the

crowd and, come what may, pushes her way to the place resounding with the voice of wisdom. On her right a grandfather and grandson sit next to a fogged-up window.

"And who wrote *Carmen?*"

"Bizet."

"And who else?"

"Mérimée."

"Who else?"

"Shchedrin."

"And the parable of those invited to the feast was painted by whom?"

"Rembrandt."

"Full name!"

"Van Rijn, Harmenszoon."

"Tell me, I beg you, who are you?" Ophelia Feliksivna bends down to the old man, greatly moved.

"I Am Solomon Moiseyevich Bass," He Replies

"WHY ARE YOU HERE AND NOT IN LOS ANGELES?"

In response Bass grants a smile brimming with wisdom, cunning, and not entirely comprehensible love.

The folks wedged in the aisles are exchanging the wryest of words that they have ever heard on the street. The trolley-bus vibrates. Its windows are spattered with mud. No one can see what's going on outside or where he is at the present moment. The doors won't open. The brawl has swollen to maximum capacity and is in danger of bursting at any moment into a fiery self-annihilating war. The old are ready to fight the young, the dark-haired the blonds, the squab the lanky; those who paid bus fare feel fully within their rights to wallop the freeloaders, those who believe in lists want to make mincemeat out of those who stake their lives on the merits of lines, those in the back would do battle with those up front, the standing will dig their nails into the seated, and he who is on top shall trample him who has fallen.

"I can't go on like this!" Ophelia Feliksivna cries into Bass's ear. "In this atmosphere of militant vulgarity! If you only knew how I suffer when I see and hear things like this! The concept of legality is utterly nonexistent! Lawlessness parades as law. The people have become accustomed to lies. And finally, take a look at this sinful, black-hearted, and helpless lot. Punish them! And tell me, what should I do?"

"Run!" Solomon Moiseyevich Bass says to her.

"When?"

"Now."

"Today?"

"Immediately."

"But explain to me, please, how can I do this physically?" asks Ophelia Feliksivna. "It's a long way to the door. The bus won't stop. And if they figure out that I've decided to jump ship, they will take me and bind me by my hands and feet. Wouldn't it be better, wouldn't it be wiser to wait out this storm, and then, let's say, tomorrow . . ."

"Fine," says Bass, "let it happen tomorrow."

"Oh, thank you! Thank you!" Ophelia Feliksivna clings to the Teacher's arm. "How well I understand you! But, on the other hand, is it really possible to get ready in a day? I'm speaking, of course, not of clothing or earthly wares that fall prey to the ravages of moths, mice, and woodworms. Do you think it's easy to come up to them and throw in their faces: 'Good-bye, I'm going, I'm not one of you anymore, I belong to Bass!'? I'd have to spend at least a week preparing for something like that."

"All right," says Bass. "If you need a week, take a week."

"To renounce everything and begin anew!" Ophelia Feliksivna shakes her not-yet-gray curls. "Based on flat, two-dimensional, simplistic decisions. To completely disregard antinomy and the dialectic. To leave behind all dualism, skepticism and doubts, ambivalence and multifariousness.

As well as the privilege of never completely belonging to anything or anybody. For what? For a promised sense of completeness and at-oneness with all being . . . Will a month from now be too late?"

"You can do it in a month," Solomon Moiseyevich answers.

"Just don't think," she tells him, "that I don't appreciate the full meaning of this. And what will happen to the chosen ones (if you only knew how grateful I am!) who spurn such an honor. And what fate awaits this trolleybus with its passengers, who, for all their squabbling, were incapable of leaving even a few congruent phrases to remember them by. Who will ever hear them or know why their hearts ached, where their treasure is buried, or that once upon a time they laughed heartily or wailed in fervent prayer? But I'm referring to something else. Let's assume I decide to go. A number of questions will immediately be raised in certain establishments. Well, first of all, they'll say, prove to us that this Solomon Moiseyevich Bass is really your direct blood relation. And second, they'll say, we, of course, know full well what kind of invitation this is (because we're not stupid!), and we could generate little papers like this for ourselves by the kilo if we wanted to. But we're not doing that. Why? Because we know—that place out there is not for people like us. What would we do with that part of ourselves that doesn't have even a drop, an inkling, of experience in that fair and noble world? How are we to conceal our twisted, deformed, tenfold sinful and clogged (you better believe it!) former lives? And if indeed everything there, on the other side, is the way that some have described it to us, then there's no bloody chance that anybody (for love or money!) is going to let us in. But what if it's all just someone's tall tale, foul lies, a provocation? Then all the more, to hell with it!—it's mu-u-u-ch cozier for us here. Because one way or another we've settled in, adjusted, we even kind of like the sights, the sounds, the smells . . .

"Of course," Ophelia Feliksivna vows, "I myself categorically reject such logic and its worldview. But I wanted to ask you. If, let's say, I was not to settle this question immediately, but a year from now, would that not be too late? What do you think?"

She hears no answer. The bus brakes violently, the passengers are thrown to the floor, and the driver, before making his escape, announces that the vehicle has broken down and it's every man for himself.

"Solomon Moiseyevich!" Ophelia Feliksivna calls out. But Bass is nowhere to be seen. The frenzied mob splinters the bus, rips its way out through every possible crack, and throws Ophelia Feliksivna out on the tattered snow.

"Run! Make your choice! But do not look back!" She hears his voice, looks back, and sees how at the site of the accident a group of deaf-mutes are pummeling each other's bloody faces, silently, without a single curse or shout.

Ophelia Feliksivna senses her stomach slowly sink, and her arms and legs turn numb until she can no longer feel them.

Lyonia Spichek Relinquishes His Cardboard, and While the Editors Seek Out Spelling Mistakes in His Schema, He Squeezes the Hand of Vitya Maliatko

YOU COULD HIDE A BRICK IN LYONIA'S HARD PALM, WHILE Vitya's can hold no more than a three-kopeck bun. The lecture-turned-article that Vitya, it seems, is about to start translating any minute now concerns the judicious use of solar energy. Its author, a California engineer, proposes the installation of solar batteries in swimming pools. This would enable us to reduce energy consumption 15 to 16 percent from current levels! The article concludes with a list of local and regional banks delighted to offer reduced-rate loans and is followed by the addresses of contractors eager to upgrade your villa roof (in record time and under budget!) with a swimming pool and sauna.

Vitya shoves the conference materials on quality issues into the drawer and regrets not having made his lunchtime escape to join the ranks of freewheeling artists. Suddenly his eyes meet those of Ophelia Feliksivna. She is pressed against the window and apparently has seen something quite out of the ordinary in the street, something with brimstone and fire, something one would not be amiss in calling a miracle. Because what else, what other acute and deeply felt emotion, could have stopped Ophelia Feliksivna so dead in her tracks?

Vitya rams his chair back and in a few quick bounds finds himself at the window. The view, however, reveals nothing momentous. Quite the opposite, in fact. As always happens at this hour, clamorous hordes of unruly schoolkids meander homeward. Senior citizens puff by, focused intently on their shopping routes. Their younger contemporaries race to their destinations with equal resolve. Some have donned everything foreign-made, causing them to believe they were tailor-made of expensive material and thus entitled to a well-stocked and colorful future. But Vitya, as a man of art, can see how they are all the same color as this drab and long ago washed-out landscape, a part and parcel of it till the day they die.

"How can one expect," Vitya asks, "that signals from higher spheres will reach down here? And what, if not these signals, is to feed the real artists and geniuses of humanity?"

Of course, there are the four elements. If they're not polluted yet. But such places probably can't be found in our parts anymore. And what remains outside of that? People and the false world of their petty relations. Best to steer clear of them!

The more Vitya presses his forehead against the glass, the more clearly he sees that everything in this busy and seemingly accidental composition is hopelessly locked in, its outcome predetermined and tied to a goal, routine, and function for all time. So where, then, is pure impulse to spring from? Or form, torn loose from necessity? Or pure color?

"I'm done for, I'm done for!" he suddenly concludes. "Five solid days of slavery per week! How many masterpieces could be painted in that time! But will they give you a chance?! They'll do everything to stop you from growing into a world-class artist. To transform a prodigy into a miserable clerk. Destroy the personality. If not maim it, then at least give it a good fright. Cut off the route to what is genuine and real."

Vitya Maliatko remembers that on Monday he received a card from the draft board, in which they invite him for the second time to bring along his passport and sign up for reserve officer training. Vitya is afraid of military service. He suspects that they want to ship him out to the Turkestan desert so that he can jump out of airplanes with a parachute. That is why he gave his mother the appropriate instructions, and why for several days now, upon hearing the doorbell ring in the evening, he runs to hide out on the balcony. But, you know, they could round up a company of soldiers and police and show up at work! Then it really will be good-bye Charlie for him!

Vitya's despair crawls over to the wet, scraggly trees lining the street, to the transit vehicles, to the still and unstill life walking around contemplating or, alternatively, just dumbly standing there or rolling around on the ground. There it is—this whole causally and historically determined world tied into knots of interconnections and dependencies and twitching ever so mildly and sporadically. And there's no getting away from it. And what's worse, not a ray of hope.

But suddenly Vitya Maliatko sees a boy turn the corner from Fifty-sixth Anniversary Street to Partisan Lymonchenko Street. A young man. He carries his body with obvious pleasure, his movements so light and assured, as though his limbs were in fact not tied by countless invisible strings (that is to say: thoughts, obligations, worries, and so on) to that which always pulls to the bottom. It's as though someone had lifted this weight off him. It's as if he not only woke up this morning but was born anew—a young, fully developed man, and even wearing soft, stylish briefs. How about that! He walks the familiar landscape but does not twitch in unison with it. You see that?!

Vitya, too, straightens out his shoulders. The boy walks on, smiling. He's probably just heard something pleasant. Or got himself a pair of imported jeans. No, his pants are regular, could have even been sewn at home out of cheap canvas. They're a little narrow for today's fashions, and kind of old. The color is soft, though, a pale ochre born of sunlight and regular washing.

Vitya Maliatko remembers where he first saw this boy. It was summertime, at the terminal stop of the streetcar line. There used to be a kiosk there where a one-armed lush sold cigarettes. He never asked for your age (Vitya used to go there with his buddy, also in grade 7), because he never gave you change. And so one sunny day they each got themselves a pack of Bulgarian Jebelas, jumped on the Number 27, bounced into two empty seats, and it was here that Vitya found himself side by side with a boy perhaps five years older than himself. A painter's box hung over his shoulder on a strap, and his fingers were stained with paint. The artist's eyes were glued to the window, and his face carried a blissful smile. But try as he might, Vitya could see nothing on the other side of the glass to inspire such enchantment. He'd obviously thought up something warm and cozy for himself, and was now drawing pleasure from it. If indeed "thinking" had any part in it. Vitya Maliatko and his buddy hopped off the tram a few stops later, while the other fellow, bewitched, no doubt rode to the end of the line, where he was booted off by the foul-mouthed driver, a veritable black hag.

And isn't it something that now, after what seems like so many years, Vitya would, first, recognize that boy and, second, realize why, in the midst of all the bustle back then, that boy had been struck speechless. It was because, Vitya now understood, at that riveting moment the artist in canvas pants had been able to feel and absorb signals (also known as vibrations) from the higher spheres! And to unite, even if only for a moment, with the four elements: water, fire, earth, and air, from which all pure colors and perfect forms are derived! And that's where he's headed now, rapt in such inspiration!

And So Vitya Drops Everything and Runs After the Artist

THE LATTER DOESN'T NOTICE HIM. HE'S JUST FINISHED HIS shift at work, where he hauled boxes of Sunshine margarine from the grocery store basement for several hours and then fought off the embraces of his companion-in-labor, Lyosha. Lyosha absolutely insisted that he help him crack a flask of the strong pink stuff and wouldn't lay off until the artist finally lied about undergoing treatment for the clap.

And here he is, finally, soaring homeward, aquiver with the thought of inhaling the narcotic scent of oil paints, for it was for their sake that he, unlike Vitya Maliatko, parted ways with Soviet employment and divorced his wife.

Several years imbued with the creative quest have trickled by and evaporated somewhere since then. After picking up his employment passbook, he set out immediately for the village of Votylivka, where, as he was secretly told by the mural painter from whom he took lessons, there were some people from the Ternopil region working on the construction of a barn. They had made some discreet inquiries about master painters who might be willing to do the interior of their village church.

The artist walks up to them and introduces himself. They stare at him, round-eyed: What church? The artist explains how he found out about it. Now their terror is absolute: What does this easterner want from them? They've never heard of a mural painter, and no, they did not collect money for a church nor did they covertly lay concrete blocks on mortar in the middle of the night, because they live in an entirely different village altogether.

Really? The artist doesn't believe them (he renounced his former life for this!).

Definitely! The villagers, who have been around the block more than once, twinkle back at him from under their furrowed brows.

And so unraveled the plan in which his art instructor was to supervise this godly and lucrative work, and he was to be the chief assistant.

The artist returns to the city and quarrels with the mural painter, who happens to be a member of the party and, having put great effort into getting where he is today, has no wish to lose it all because of somebody's juvenile dreams. The artist tries to get a job as a graphic designer, to perhaps make posters for the theater or a club and work on his art late at night. But wherever he turns they seem to need draftsmen, and he only got a C in drafting. The only one in his whole transcript, by the way. And so he becomes a freight handler, after first paying the directress a bribe, since, legally, she has no right to accept someone with a higher education for this position.

In the evenings he paints. The lines and colors, however, are in no hurry to congregate in pleasant patterns on the surfaces prepared for them. On the contrary, they reveal their capricious natures every chance they get. Gentle and mild-mannered paints crawl out of their tubes and get into senseless quarrels without the slightest provocation. First they demand private space allocation, then they want some kind of admixtures. That color happens to be their enemy, this one they don't get along with. And so vengeful, too! Fuck 'em, he says, reduces everything to plain black and white, and walks right into THE TRAP. Today we may call it simplistic schematism, tomorrow it will be chaoticism, after that an attempt at naked polysemanticism, primitivism, absence of content, literariness, and lack of excess.

The artist assembles his better works and takes them to Shcherbak. Shcherbak examines them from the front, then from various angles, hems and haws for a long time, and says that it's never too late to change professions. On hearing this verdict, the artist grabs a knife, cuts and shreds the cardboard, smashes the frames, and doesn't sleep all night. In the morning, looking at the blue rings under his eyes from the sleepless night, he asks himself: Who the hell is this Shcherbak anyway? What has he created that would make me take him seriously?! And he breaks off all relations with him. And also with the guy who introduced him. And with his new girlfriend, a student of the Faculty of Architecture (oh, if only Vitya had even an ounce of his decisiveness!). And, as long as he was at it, with his position as a loader in the grocery store.

But life does not stand still. He does not get a new job, he does get a new wife, and he feverishly searches for his own unique style. Who the hell ever said, he fumes rebelliously, that art has to portray reality? That's nonsense!

And so begins the next abstract period in his art. "Do clouds maintain a stable form, once and for all defined?" he asks his wife. "Or water? Or the flames of an open fire? Huh?"

His wife keeps silent. She has a job in day care and brings home two full pots of special-diet food each day. Her husband has an ulcer, you see.

Some time later he becomes disillusioned with his new approach and returns to the rhetorical questions. "Tell me, whom or what do I paint for?" he assails his wife. "Just to express myself? When you really get right down to it, who needs me?"

She tells him that she does, hugs him, and holds him close, but at that moment their sick child wakens abruptly with a persistent and not very healthy-sounding cough.

"Only to repeat that which already exists just as well without me?" he continues.

"Quiet!" his wife snaps back.

"What's it all about?" He doesn't understand. "That which we see already has its own unique God-given form that nobody can go beyond anyway! To create something just to sell? Fine. Let it be that."

He packs up his favorite paintings and goes to the market square. Nobody's buying. That's because the masses haven't reached his level yet, he tells himself. He shows his best work to Fursa. Fursa wrinkles his nose. "I understand what you're doing," he says, "I even approve of the underlying concept, but the final product does not, either compositionally or in terms of color . . . "

The artist runs out of the basement where Fursa, genius of the paintbrush, has sipped tea and spun his web for decades, being thoroughly unknown in either the East or the West.

"I don't care," he assures himself. "I sneeze, spit, and shit on everything this gnome has to say! I will create in spite of them, I will draw strength from their failure to recognize me, from my loneliness. I will break off relations with everyone, but I will break through!"

He does just that. For he sees how the bonds of family and the chains of production block his artistic regeneration, don't let him feel the breathing of all creation.

But it's something else that's interesting. No sooner does he break out of the siege and clear away the space, time, heart, and mind for art than suddenly other relationships with their sticky tentacles of new links and even more inappropriate thoughts begin to pry their way in. Because there's a law of nature at work here that cannot tolerate a vacuum.

The next chunk of time goes by. The artist has left the

city with its poisonous emissions, alimony payments, and residence permits. He now lives at the edge of a forest that is moving in on the village. The people are all gone. The river, which once gave them sustenance, was dammed up, and the reservoir has swallowed most of the empty houses. Artists live here nowadays, in tents, deserted buildings, and out in the open air in the summer. The wells have grown over, but streams trickle through the gullies. There are plenty of mushrooms and blackberries in the forest. The abandoned gardens will grow nobody's sweet fruits and vegetables for a long time to come. And they do bring in bread to the nearest living village, even if it is only once a week. There's lots of good clay in the river, and you can find materials to build a kiln for pottery. The women artists on hand have long since rejected old-world prejudice and are willing to embrace happiness. In other words, it would seem that, well, what could possibly get in the way of creative ecstasy?! A complete union with the vibrations. When content has found the form and pulls you along. And all the obstacles have fallen. And everything is about to reveal itself to you in its true nature.

However, one day just before sunset, a colony of Krishnas draped in their sheets crawled out from the city to join them. Their head man, Guru O. K. (Oleh Kharytonovych, used to work as a psychologist in the Pedagogy NII, but never did get his Ph.D.), commanded his followers to set up an ashram there. In their wake, battle-ready militiamen began hopping out of paddy wagons amid clouds of dust, with an experienced officer of state security at their helm. It didn't matter who you were—nonconformist, painter, disciple of the Gita, yogi, ceramic potter, ethnographer, or humble vacationer in nature's bosom—everybody got hauled off. Only the artist was saved, sitting as he was on a mulberry tree that evening, trying in vain to capture the local orange sunset with a plain lead pencil.

"Oh, hateful society!" he recited several times. "I curse

you. You and your lackeys! Wherever you are, your tentacles are sure to reach out after us. And it's they that turn a creator into a maggot, a grub, a cripple!"

He climbed down from the tree and perhaps for the first time in his life stood face to face with a world in which, no matter how far you cast your glance, there were no two-legged creatures.

And so he steps onto a path (it's as though someone's pulling him!) and begins an arduous climb up the hill. An oak tree stands on top, beneath it rests a shady spot, and in the middle is a point where three elements—water, air, earth—converge. And if you light a fire, you've got another. Because a stream flows through here. And you can see the river. The earth is soft, sticky, and warm. And the air so rarefied and transparent it becomes a superconductor for cosmic ideas and pulsations.

The artist builds a campfire and notices a fox scratching its way to the pinnacle, right under his feet, twisting and turning and rubbing its rump against the ground in a way that is not entirely clear: is it defecating or dancing? Before such impertinence would have caused him to whack the fox with a stick, but now, at this particular spot, animal gestures reveal their meaning to him. And he understands that behind these actions stands not contempt for him as a creative artist, but rather a wood tick that has attached itself to the mammal and is rapidly swelling from its blood. But he does not condemn the tick either, for the tick is governed by a genuine natural instinct that reconciles and balances the needs of all life. That's what makes the world go round, a blessed, all-encompassing, seamless, and gapless world without end.

"Enough sitting around! Go for it!" the timely thought pounds at the artist's skull. "Paint something, anything! While it's still naked and granted you unconditionally. What you seize right now will last you a lifetime. A chance like this may not come again."

"Calm down," the other organs tell the head. "Why don't you just sit back, absorb it all, and celebrate?"

"You must work," the head prickles. "Letting something like this go is a sin and a crime!"

"But you can't capture it!" the other organs explain, still in bliss. "And with what? Don't tell us you want take on perfection? What for? One false move here and instant gratification is gone forever."

In the middle of this conclusion the artist is accosted by Vitya Maliatko with his inane questions. It takes him a long time to understand what this punk wants from him. How is he supposed to know whether the guy has talent, whether he can become a world-famous painter, or if it's smarter to stick with NIIAA and stay put?

Vitya sees that the artist cannot get off the mountain and that at the same time he is edging, like a sleepwalker, into the path of an oncoming trolley. From the other side a police cruiser advances on him, blaring something authoritative from the bullhorn on its roof. It's difficult to piece together a coherent message from the verbal fragments, and therefore wiser to get off the road and hide behind a pillar or tree.

Vitya Maliatko tries to convey to the artist that in principle he's all for it. No ifs, ands, or buts, in thought and in deed. It's just that at this precise moment it would probably be safer to forgo the world of illusion and wait until things cool down a bit.

"And also," he says, "I'd like to get an answer from you regarding my artistic potential, present and future."

"I am getting so sick of you," interrupts the artist, by this time seriously annoyed.

Vitya Maliatko, not anticipating this blow (what's the matter with him?!) turns on his heels and retreats in the direction of the fifth floor. A stern answer crashes like a sledgehammer through the invisible fanfares behind him.

Make up your mind! On your own! Now!

While the Women Are Proofing the Words, Lyonia Spichek Strolls from Desk to Desk

HE MAKES AWKWARD BUT QUITE SINCERE AND WELL-MEANING overtures to the women with questions like "Well, what about here?" "How's this here?" "Working hard, huh?"—which are, in fact, simply a case of trying to be friendly and require no answer.

Someone calls and hangs up. Ophelia Feliksivna huffs indignantly. Svitlana Zhuravlynchenko blushes deeply. And the more desperately she instructs herself, "Do not lose your natural coloring under any circumstances! Hang on to that swarthiness for dear life!" the redder she gets. All present notice this and draw their conclusions.

"Look at them," grumbles Zoyka, piqued at whole group. "Everybody's got residence status but me! It's not fair! This isn't even serfdom, it's slavery!"

The lust for freedom gives birth to a plan of how to get living space quickly and independently of NIIAA. She must, without losing a moment, pop by the dorm, take off her everyday gear, put on that brand-new, never-once-worn dress, and run over to her aunt's, so that the latter can see what a hardworking niece she's got.

Zoyka knitted this dress several times. All by herself, without a pattern, prompted only by her heart. She had once torn it out from a women's magazine and hidden it somewhere, except now she can't remember where. The concept was a simple one—shift dress, raglan sleeves, stocking stitch (right side, knit; wrong side, purl), and ribbing for cuffs, collar, and trim. Originality, compositional beauty, quick execution, guaranteed success. Life, however, deemed otherwise. She wanted to make stylish raglan shoulders, on an angle—it didn't work. She had to unravel everything and settle for square-cut drop sleeves. She wanted to pretty it up with popcorn stitching, but miscounted the loops and had to throw out the whole piece. She had this great idea of knitting a cable down the sleeve, except that everything went diagonally all to hell. So she unraveled the whole thing, threw it in the drawer, came down with strep throat in the process, and then one day picked up the knitting needles again out of boredom and, without any fancy tricks but with plenty of howls and curses, finished off the damned knitting in time for Revolution Day, bringing the stocking stitch all the way up to the throat and leaving it at that.

That's it. Over to visit the aunt right away! Drop in, find out how life's been treating her. Then flash the new dress in front of her and ask: Well, do you think it's terrific or just so-so? And only then tell her who made it.

The aunt, of course (Zoyka can already imagine what it's going to be like), bugs out her eyes (she hasn't bought herself anything new in a hundred years) and gets upset.

"You couldn't find anything worse than that?" she asks.

Her niece has her pride, too, and answers that that's the style now.

"And how much," the old woman wants to know, "did this marvel cost you?"

"Forty rubles," says Zoyka.

"Fo-orty ru-u-bles?!?!" The aunt's spectacles fall to her knees and from there to the floor. "For forty rubles . . . I could . . . !!!" The aunt quakes, drops down on all fours, and moves her hands back and forth along the floor for a long time until she finally retrieves her borrowed eyes. Strands of gray hair hang from her sleeves, coated generously with globs of dust off a floor long since washed, on which you could find every imaginable object. "I could get you ten dresses for that money!!!"

"Oh, what are you saying, Auntie?" Zoyka can no longer keep up the pretense.

"What am I saying?!" Auntie can no longer keep down her anger. "What am I saying?! Living too high on the hog!"

"I'm living too high!?" Zoyka begins to cry. "You're talking about me?!?"

"Who else!" the aunt chokes on her spittle.

"I haven't had soap for a week!" Zoyka Vereshchak tries to explain her position.

"We didn't have soap either when we were young!" her aunt informs her. "No soap! No coats! No boots!"

"And what, do I have boots?!" Zoyka runs out to the corridor and returns to shove her dirty, never-once-polished galoshes under her aunt's nose. "I only got myself a coat in my fourth year of university!" she says.

"And I," the aunt strikes back, "never had such an opportunity, to study at a university, although now, thanks to the fascist attack on the Fatherland, I'm a life member of the Cause!"

"Good for you!" sobs Zoyka, who in her fourteen years of faithful service to the Komsomol never got a single decoration or perk. Biting her lips blood red, she tumbles with a splash into the murky waters of hysteria, not without some satisfaction.

The aunt carefully observes the results of her pedagogical methods, gives Zoyka her handkerchief, and hugs and comforts her. "There, there, that's enough," she says approvingly, "only the dead are ever completely satisfied."

"Register me in your apartment!" Zoyka says to her.

"Why?" The aunt is honestly surprised. "I won't be dying for a while."

"Live as long as you like and good health to you!" Zoyka quickly finds the right thing to say. "But it's bound to happen someday. Why should family property go to waste?"

"Go on," the aunt commands.

"I'm tired of being dependent on everybody," confesses her niece.

"So that's what it's all about!" The aunt draws the only possible conclusion. "Don't tell me a tiny insect like yourself wants freedom, too? There's not enough trouble with cockroaches and broken toilets to keep you busy?! You want to take on the world! You're sure you won't get a hernia while you're at it?"

Zoyka, however, is not flustered by these words, but instead continues to fight for her right as an albeit small individual, but an individual all the same, to freedom of personal choice.

"And do you fully understand," the aunt is alarmed, "what you have gone after in your greed? And what kind of life you are condemning yourself to?"

"Yes!" Zoyka proudly returns her gaze. "But was it not for this that my Grandfather Pervomay Vereshchak fought?! May his holy ideals be ever venerated!"

"I don't ever want to see your face here again!" the aunt hisses at her.

"Get me registered!" Zoyka pleads. "Give me a chance to live like a human being!"

"Why, certainly!" the aunt promises, and without much ado leaps on top of the poor girl. Her stiff, highly merited mustache cuts the air like a whip, but Zoyka Vereshchak dodges, slips behind the toilet bowl, and finds refuge between the pail and pipe.

Of course, it was difficult for her at first, because that's what the times were like. Especially when it came to food and shelter. Well, and with supplies, too, that goes without saying. And it would have been quite improper to expect the others to pitch in and help. She just had to manage. A slightly bit-into apple that someone threw away here, a crust of bread there, and in the garbage some wet tea leaves, or else a pretty wrapper. But we're not the type to perish. We'll make it through!

And what kind of personal life can one speak of in these conditions? You were left to your own devices, delving deep inside for self-fulfillment. She went to the library often. Why don't you go, why don't you go, everyone would coach her, and tell them, "I have a legal right." And let them all be ashamed that they're not looking after you like the apple of their eye, that their hearts aren't bleeding seeing you like this!

She goes. She walks in. Wearing the same pants as always, wide cuffs, almost transparent in several spots.

"I need a place!" she says. "I've worked every possible assignment and position for you!"

She begins to list her various posts.

"We don't have any," they interrupt.

"And what about a conscience, you have that?" she insists.

"Only in theory," they tell her.

"How can that be?" She can't stop herself. "I've always performed in a timely and efficient manner. I've never touched a perk or junket, spent my whole life crawling around in shit. Perhaps in my youth I may have expressed some disappointment, but then I calmed down and learned to love it. Give me a place, I beg you, I can't stand it anymore! Oh, how I . . . "

"Away with her!" She hears the heartless verdict. "And keep whacking her with a stick until you drive her right off the premises."

"Oh, how I hate you all!" Fearless Zoyka's blood is aflame.

"Gag her! Don't let her tell the truth!" They cut her short. "And what do you think you know, you two-bit squeak?! If we didn't keep you working like a dog day and night, and didn't give you a good scare every once in a while, you'd be as lazy as a slug! You'd just lie there, slobber, and shit right in your bed! We know the likes of you!"

"If my Grandpa Comrade Pervomay suddenly walked in here . . . " Zoyka throws the truth right into their faces.

"Shut up!" The enemy spatters her with venom and bears down on her throat.

" . . . my Grandpa Vereshchak!" wheezes Zoyka. "Then the judgment of history . . . clean hands . . . immaculate descendants . . . the proud name of a hero . . . "

She tries to free her gentle larynx and, still in the grip of passion, bumps into a monumental, bluntly posed question.

"And where, ducky, did you get the idea" they ask her, "that you're entitled to be sheltered and fed?"

"What do you mean?" Zoyka doesn't follow. "Then why did my grandfather lay down his short, overwhelmingly heroic life? For the good of everyone. And if there isn't enough for everyone, then at least so that I'd have enough, his granddaughter by blood. Because that's way of the flesh."

"Oh!" The aunt can't stand it (for it was she who was executing Zoyka's strangulation) and falls to the floor with a thud.

Such a turn of events seriously bewilders Zoyka Vereshchak. How could the bestial enemy have turned into her very own aunt so adroitly?

"What is it, what's going on?" she demands.

"Don't ask!" gasps the aunt.

"Why not? I want the truth. Justice. An apartment."

"No!"

"Explain, at least!"

"I can't!"

"Why?"

"You won't be able to take it."

"I can take anything!"

"Swear it!"

"I swear!"

"All right then, listen!"

The aunt bows down to the ground, rubs her eyes, yawns deeply again and then again, and begins to know all, understand all, and have power over all. She parts her lips and tells the truth.

"It happened in such and such a place," she says, and gives the exact date. "In secret from you and craving the triumph of justice in the distribution of living space, I entered a deposition in which, on the basis of concrete facts, I asked the relevant people, why is it that some of us are pressed against the wall, barely keeping body and soul together, while others live sumptuously on the fat of the land? Give me a principled reply, I said, whereas I am the daughter of Pervomay Vereshchak!

"They summon me to the *relevant establishment* immediately. I stand there, freezing at the pass dispensation wicket. An officer, burdened heavily by the apple of bitter knowledge, as I figured out later, comes down and leads me to the basement. I sign an oath of secrecy, and they bring out from the vault a book published by Vaillis in the West: *Vereshchak Without the Smokescreen and Dust*.

"Feel free to acquaint yourself, they say.

"No, I say.

"It's an order, they say.

"What was I to do? The content of what I read still pounds inside my head. Here it is.

"Pervomay Vereshchak is not a hero. He was nowhere near the zones of combat and heroic deed. As a most despicable double-crossing traitor to the Fatherland, he spent his entire wild and stormy youth in a root cellar, to which he periodically enticed inexperienced ladies on political assignment, by means of a distinctive whistle and scent. In other words, his underground activity was destructive and directed against the people. This is corroborated by objective analyses of several independent and in-no-way-connected bald professors, and by secret facts in Western archives that fell into the hands of our allies under mysterious circumstances.

"Here's an excerpt, the comrades from the vault say to me. Take a look, please.

"Everything is swimming before my eyes. They wheel up a stool, sit me down, find the appropriate page, and begin to read.

"P. V. (Pervomay Vereshchak) *never* (the italics were theirs) took up the flaming torch from the hand of Comrade Budonny. He acquired his glorious surname in exchange for a set of epaulets, which he, in fact, stole from Burya the orderly (that character, by the way, is a figment of the author's imagination) while the latter was still not quite out of the clutches of a severe hangover. The so-called 'final courageous feat of Vereshchak' is a fraud. Vaillis has marshaled compelling evidence to prove that P. Vereshchak was a raging heterosexual. As it turns out, he not only never threw his bloodied body into enemy machine-gun fire, never inflamed hearts and minds with the cause of collective farming, did not stand at the head of a guerrilla unit bearing his name, but, quite the contrary, spent the whole time inventing slogans of morally dubious and at times even overtly subversive character. A day before the 'courageous feat,' he was sighted in a village on Cherry Hill. Barefoot, clad only in his briefs, he would approach better-off households, scratch at the door, and, shoving the residents aside, would head straight for the pantry to guzzle down all the colognes and aftershaves. The peasants, quickly changing into workers' clothing, set up an ambush, captured him, bound him in wrapping material, and handed him over to the Germans as part of the traditional bread-and-salt greeting. The Germans, not believing their luck, get in touch with Berlin. Berlin is in complete panic. A secret memo arrives: Dispatch the 'parcel' to us for analysis immediately by train in an unmarked car. However, the diagnosis findings and autopsy results have thus far not been located. We assume that the trail leads to the jungles of northern Paraguay or to the coffers of counterintelligence agencies.

"However, Vaillis hints, a troika may have been summoned to investigate the case of Vereshchak. The text of its decision regarding the inadvisability of public dissemination of pertinent facts has obviously not been preserved. We have only the outline of a project on the importance of propaganda work among the masses. But it is not impossible that on that very day, through channels of telephone communication, the local government office may have received an unofficial recommendation regarding the de-Vereshchakization of the regional history museum. And that means, among other things, specifically, that if some pensioner, regardless of how glorious a surname she bears (glorious only to a point, of course!), if that pensioner suddenly begins to yap needlessly or lay claim to *special privileges,* then we are ready to open her eyes to the truth in very short order. And we may even publish her name as a direct descendant of the crook, tramp, and vagabond Lymonchenko."

"No!" Zoyka throws herself to the floor to make her point. "What about the Stand of Glory?"

"Delusion!" croaks the aunt, overcoming a spasm. "Treachery and deceit."

"And Voulia? Don't tell me she, too . . . "

"A common whore!" the aunt must confess.

"God, I wish I didn't know," Zoyka whispers in a voice transformed beyond recognition. "I'd rather be deaf, my ears plugged with yellow wax forever."

"I warned you, didn't I?" the aunt reminds her. "And this isn't all yet. They lead me up the stairs from the basement, shattered by grief, give me some papers to sign, and let me out. How do I go on living, I ask myself, knowing what I know? But the heavily bugged walls were silent. I don't know how everything would have turned out if not for one elderly, good-hearted cleaning woman. While all those boorish security guards were thinking about women and days off, she quietly pulled out an even more secret file from the classified drawer and, hiding it under her apron, showed it to me. It was a special secret dossier on Pervomay Vereshchak!

"In that dossier I read that the aforementioned monograph by Vaillis never came out in the West. It was published right there, in that basement, with the purpose of further throwing potential enemies off track. The real author is none other than our hero-colonel Krutykh!"

"And what about Vereshchak?" Zoyka can't stand the suspense.

" . . . a fictional character made up by Krutykh, who was himself executed by firing squad according to the will of the people!" The aunt loses the rest of her self-control and clutches Zoyka's throat.

"Register me!" Zoyka can barely breathe out the words. "For I am no longer the granddaughter of a hero. At least, after you die, let the apartment go to me and not this lying, thieving state . . . "

"No!" grimaces the aunt.

"Why not?" Zoyka faints.

"You don't deserve it!" the aunt explains. "The minute that stamp lands on your papers you'll be off to parties day and night! And what if I die?"

"Quite the opposite!" the niece tries to convince her. "You'll have no need to do that if I'm always by your side."

"And what if you go to work?"

"I won't go. I'll get sick leave and look after you."

"And if they don't give it to you?"

"They will! There's a special ordinance to that effect."

"An ordinance? There's no more Pervomay, and you expect some kind of ordinance to be honored? I know you! You've waited just long enough for me to get removed from the Stand of Glory. I shall not let you bespittle the great ideals!"

And so, by moving her hand successively from the throat to the mouth and nose of her niece, the aunt succeeds in closing off the air passage.

"Don't let me die!" wails Zoyka. "Let me go! Give me a tiny place. I'll never do it again!"

"You have to earn it first," answers the aunt, but, calming down, releases the air passage a little. Enough for Zoyka to swallow some house dust and learn her fate.

"Well?" The aunt looks deep into her eyes. "What will it be? You want the truth? Freedom? Or would you rather leave things the way they are? Answer me! It's your choice!"

*Finally Lyonia Takes the Cardboard with All the Words
Proofread by the Women (Although He Could Have Saved
Himself the Trouble of Dragging It Around, A Piece of Paper
with Text Would Have Done Just as Well), and Together with
Lupova Departs from Room 507*

AT THE DOOR THEY MEET UP WITH KHLOPITZ, BOWING deeply. Khlopitz is a mathematician and head of the mathematical section. Ophelia Feliksivna, who happens to be dialing her friend Agnesa Lucianivna at this moment, inquires of Khlopitz in universally recognizable gestures whether it's she he's come to see. Khlopitz whirls his arms like a dragonfly just knocked out in full flight by a tractor and explains that the article, edited last week by Ophelia's girls, has yielded several inconsistencies.

Having said this, he goes to the window, smells the cactus, asks whose caring hand nurtures the flora, and, drawing a full circle, seats himself on the edge of a chair beside Svitlana Zhuravlynchenko.

"So that's what's going on!" Zoyka Vereshchak figures it out.

Khlopitz's flirtations drive Antonina Pavlivna to the telephone. The line is busy.

"I must run to them! Save them! Before it's too late!"

But rather than jump out of Room 507 and forty minutes later draw the two men of her life to her breast, she dives into the text once again and, stumbling over heaps of "-ocities" and "-ations," rushes off in the opposite direction. To the place where she is happy and full of anticipation, where everything still lies ahead.

On graduation from high school she is cheated out of a gold medal and doesn't go to the university that year, but works instead for the department that supplies the Ministry of Inter-Five-Year-Plan Construction with elevators. At the New Year's Eve party, in the company of former schoolmates, she is introduced to Volodya Smyrnov, a student at the Polytechnical Institute. He walks her home all the way to the other end of town, then calls her, then calls her again, asks her to go see the new Franco-Italian movie starring Sophia Loren, then to other films with equally impressive actors and actresses in various roles, then to the birthday parties of his friends and concerts of popular bands and singers, like Giorgio Marianovich and The Crooners.

In the summertime, they go to the beach. After Volodya's finals, Tonya takes a short vacation from work and Volodya rents a tent. In the morning they ride in from opposite ends of the city to Riverside Station, and from there take a riverboat out to where the banks are overgrown with reeds and dense willow trees. After choosing a good spot, they pitch a tent, gather brushwood for a long time (there's just oodles of it there), and go swimming. Volodya knows how to dig a circle around the campfire so it doesn't spread, and he was able to light it with one match on his first try. He brought all the equipment for fishing, and Tonya brought all the spices for soup. At dusk they cook some oatmeal with a can of "sardines au tomate," and for dessert there is strawberry pudding. As they prepare for bed, the group camped out by the small lake in the thickets starts singing and playing the guitar, and every other word they utter is a swearword!

Volodya is becoming agitated. Tonya explains that the singing doesn't bother her at all and that she's kind of hard of hearing anyway, especially at that distance. Volodya raises his voice and presses his hands against her ears to make sure she doesn't catch all those words.

The song comes to an end. He tries to unfasten the zipper of her sleeping bag.

"Don't," she says, "calm down."

But he's not listening.

"Why are you doing this?" she says. "Are you trying to offend me?"

But he's like a crazy man.

"Are you trying to make me feel bad? What do you want

to do this for? Can you explain it to me without using your hands?"

"What for, what for!" He thrashes about. "Just stop pretending you're so naive, okay?" He is shouting.

"Do you want me to go?" She is almost in tears.

"Then why the hell did you come out here with me?" he says. "And anyway, how old are you? I've never had as much trouble with anybody as I'm having with you."

She cannot contain her despair.

The repugnant crowd in the bushes hands the guitar to a female companion, and she screeches, ripping at strings out of tune long ago.

"Well, well," says Tonya, "you have every reason to be pleased. You have succeeded in humiliating me. But only because you are three years older . . . Of course, I will never ever again . . . If I had known that you would so . . . Go join your friends . . . out there . . . Find someone who'll go do it with the first guy that comes along . . . anything . . . anywhere . . . with anybody . . . !"

"But I didn't mean that . . . ," he says, "I meant something else altogether. How can I explain it to you . . . "

"There's no need to explain anything to anybody here," she says. "I am painfully disillusioned with you. For some reason I thought you were a person very close and very dear to me, you understand, not just a friend but far, far more. Unfortunately, I made a mistake. Please, let me get through this night in peace. So that tomorrow morning we can go our separate ways. Forever."

An argument breaks out in the bush about who gets to rape the guitar next. The foulest language pounds against their ears.

"You misunderstood," he says.

She says nothing, feeling as though a part of her body has just been amputated. Not even her body, her soul. Oh, if only she could fall asleep and not wake tomorrow. Not tomorrow, nor the day after that.

"Tonya," Volodya touches her sleeping bag, calls her the most tender of names, but she is indifferent to all of it. So *that's* all he wants her for! Volodya rolls over to the far corner of the tent.

"Well, you should know," he says after a long pause, "that it's not just you that's never had . . . "

Black, sooty curses drown out his words. He grabs the ax and jumps outside.

"Volodya, Volodya darling!" she whispers, her voice suddenly vanished.

But Volodya's shadow has melted into the thick shrubbery. She tears the poker out of the ground by the campfire and runs after Volodya. She hears and soon sees him greet the drunken brood (there's three of them—two still quite young and green, seventeen or so, and the slut probably a bit older) and ask that they keep the singing down a bit.

The howling ceases immediately as the brood tries to absorb what the hell this new development with an ax is and how many more of them are out there.

Volodya and Tonya return to the tent. Each crawls into his own sleeping bag. There is a long silence.

Their enemies begin to growl again and then yowl, but this time without the musical accompaniment. If they should cut the ropes and bring the tent down in the middle of the night, then no matter how much Volodya and Tonya resist, they won't escape the trap.

Volodya rises, takes the ax. Tonya feels around and finds a knife in his knapsack. He motions for her not to make so much noise. Suddenly the screaming and squealing stop. Tonya begs him to give her weapons, too. He crawls into his corner, gets his bag, pulls out a fishing rod with a heavy lure and a bunch of hooks hanging from the end, and places it in her hand. But, thinking about it some more, he takes it away and passes her the ax.

They kneel for some time, cheek to cheek, listening to the June breeze tug at the willow branches. The deeper they pass into the night, the wilder the wind becomes. The aspens creak, dry branches snap, crack, and fall to the ground. Half an hour goes by, if not more, before some snorting is heard from the enemy camp, followed by a burst of laughter. They lower their weapons, although it's still too soon to lose one's guard.

Volodya hugs her and kisses her on the cheek.

"Don't," she says.

"Why not?"

"Because you only need me to prove yourself as a man. To add another check mark in your notebook. Pick up a little sexual experience."

But he takes his finger and places it on her lips.

"Are you afraid?" he asks.

"Yes," she says. "There are more of them. And they're hoods."

"I don't mean that," he says. "Are you afraid it's going to hurt? Or you just don't want to? Do you find me repulsive? All you have to do is say that I elicit negative emotions in you, and I promise, I'll set off from here right this minute, on foot, along the riverbank, perhaps very far away, so that we would never have to see each other again."

"On the contrary," Tonya confesses, "I don't feel anything like that or even close to that."

"Then why are you pushing me away so much?"

"I'm not pushing you away at all!" she says. "But if you had just a little more decency and willpower, you would understand me."

"I am so fed up," he yells, "with all these decencies and these willpowers!"

"Fine," she answers, "then put yourself in my place and from the height of your experience, as one would expect of a real man . . . "

"Oh," he moans, "it's the same story again, and again . . . "

And he sinks to the bottom of the tent, burying his face

into the ground. Her heart contracts and all the blood flows out of her arms and legs.

"What's wrong? Oh my God!" she says. "Did I say something to hurt you? Talk to me, I beg you. I'm sorry. What can I do, tell me, how can I make you feel better?"

"Do you think this is so easy for me?" says Volodya. "Maybe this is a lot harder for me than for you, and carries a lot more responsibility. A lot more."

"What does?" she asks.

"Help me!" he suddenly says to her. "And please, don't ask for anything."

"What are you talking about?" She is amazed. "I don't understand a thing."

But he is quiet.

Tonya hugs and caresses him from all sides, strokes his head.

"I love you," he says. There are tears in his voice. "You're my only one."

"I love you, too" she says, "very, very much." She is sobbing.

"Then let's do it together!" he whispers, unbuttoning her shirt, tearing his way through the layers of clothing, under rings of elastic, up the tensed muscles that yield and then contract again with each touch, no longer from resistance but rather from a desired union.

"Let's," she says to him, "let's! Let's!"

Outside a storm descends on the beach, on the shrubbery and the river. The wind drags birds and tents toward the water, it bends and twists sturdy trees. One sees, and shortly thereafter hears, the lightning bolts strike through plump swollen clouds stuffed with moist cotton batting.

Something Terrible May Be Happening to Them Right Now!
And I'm Sitting Here! Antonina Pavlivna Tortures Herself

"HOW I HATE THIS WORK! HOW CAN I BREAK OUT OF HERE?"

"Very simply," someone from deep inside speaks up in a familiar internal voice. Although, in the old days, under different conditions, this voice could have easily belonged to the evil spirit of temptation. And a few years later to a messenger from another planet. They say a lot of their saucers started hanging around the Earth then. They're not happy with the way earthlings live.

"In the basement," the voice continues, "where the workshops are, all the windows have bars to protect them. But the boys, Vitya Maliatko's friends, have sawed through them at various points. And if you gently press . . . "

"I wouldn't feel right . . . "

"All right. There's another way. Through the bathroom. But it's a men's room."

"They'll see me!"

"Impossible. Vitya Maliatko will stand guard."

"I'm scared."

"Well, what did you think? You have to pay for freedom! So what do you want to do, stay or go? Answer me!"

Antonina Pavlivna puts off giving an answer as best she can and looks over at the tent. She imagines she sees Ilona crawling inside. She grabs a willow switch and, leaving no footprints on the wet sand, rushes toward the tent.

"Hey, wait a minute! This wasn't part of the deal!" warns the voice.

"I have to know!" She struggles to break loose. "It's all beginning to fit together. In June he told me he was going fishing with Kucheruk. Andriy begged to come along too, but he wouldn't take him. I agreed, because it was pouring rain. I thought: Kucheruk is an obvious alcoholic. Why should the child watch something like that? And now everything's clear to me! It wasn't Kucheruk at all!"

"I'm really tired of this," says the voice. "I'm asking you for the last time: Do you want to get off work or . . . "

"Let me in!" Antonina Pavlivna tears herself free and bursts into the tent.

Volodya is lying on the ground in his sleeping bag and shaking.

Andriy is studying a newspaper fragment that he found in the bushes. It's drizzling. The wind is beating against the canvas walls. Andriy had just been out and overturned the pot of soup. Volodya gave him a good whipping.

"What did you do that for?" cries Andriy.

"Because I want you to grow up to be a man," says Volodya. "Not a bookworm, not a sissy, not a librarian! Understand?"

"Well, please don't be upset, Dad," says Andriyko, "but I can see already that I'm not going to be an engineer. I make too many mistakes in life. And I doubt I'll be an intellectual like Mother, either. Because the teacher says that I'm too restless."

"So what do you want to be?"

"I'll study to be a driver," says Andriy. "But not a truck driver, because there's too much grease and stink. Remember how I once got grease on myself when I was five years old? That's when I really found out what kind of trouble something like that can be! I almost scraped off all my skin. It went in so deep. Remember?"

"Yep."

"So, as I was saying," Andriy continues, "I considered the subway for a long time. But there are only tunnels there and nothing very interesting. So the only thing left is trolleybuses and streetcars. They're quiet, they don't pollute the air, and they also have, as I read in the paper yesterday, their own vacation resort at the seashore. You don't happen to know where that is exactly, do you?"

At night Volodya's temperature rises. "If we don't leave immediately, this will be the end of me," he decides.

In the morning it's raining. They leave the canned food and fishing gear in the grass, because they don't have the strength to carry it all now. Andriy drags his little knapsack and the tent. Volodya has to stop every twenty yards.

"Dad, Dad, you're walking awfully wobbly!" says Andriy. "You're not drunk, are you? I saw this cartoon in a magazine . . ."

Volodya shakes his head.

"I also read," says Andriy, "that you can get drunk even if you don't drink wine or beer. From the bacteria in your stomach. Once an American cowboy-rancher noticed that his cows were behaving strangely. They . . ."

Volodya gains momentum by pushing against the tree trunks and drags himself onward. There is almost no level ground, it's all up and down. Andriy bounds alongside, telling him about the Mapuche and Huilliche Indians who consume alcohol continuously from early childhood.

"But this doesn't worry me too much," he says. "You once let me sniff some liquor, remember? Now there's a revolting substance! Whoa!" he cries suddenly. "Barracuda!"

"What?" Volodya jerks up.

"A barracuda!" Andriy is pointing his finger at the sky. "It's a kind of a fish! Lives in the ocean! Like a saltwater pike. It's in the encyclopedia!"

The wind pastes tufts of cloud into outlandish figures, clears away the mist, breaks through the barrier that wants to divide the world into earth and sky.

They get as far as the ditch that marks the beginning of the climb up the hill, from which the village, the river, and the boats can be seen. Volodya sits on the ground for half an hour. It's hard for him to see the sun and pure color through his tears.

"And did you know," Andriy asks, "that everything is shifting around right now? Very soon, in another couple thousand years, the geographical North Pole will be pointing not at the North Star but at one of the stars in the constellation Orion! I forget exactly which one."

They begin their ascent and two hours later step onto the pier. Volodya collapses on a bench.

"I'd give anything to be there with you!" Antonina Pavlivna cries out to her husband and son. "But it's just not possible!"

"You know how the individual Indo-European languages came into being?" Andriy asks Volodya. "Do you? No? Once upon a time there lived these nations, and then the Indo-Europeans came along . . . But you're not listening! Oh, here comes the hydrofoil! Hurry up! Come on! We can go! Are you coming or not? Mom!" Andriy suddenly turns to her. "Why are you sitting there? Let's go! We're waiting!"

Antonina Pavlivna wants to rise up toward him, but she faints. If not for the institutional desk and chair, her body would surely have slid to the floor, melted into a large puddle, and then, in accordance with the laws of physics, turned into light warm vapor and floated up to the soaring clouds.

"And What Other Inconsistencies Have You Found There?"
Meows Ophelia Feliksivna in an Atypically High Voice

"NOT YOU, NOT YOU!" SHE EXPLAINS TO AGNESA LUCIANIVNA in the telephone receiver. "It's something at work here."

"So it was you, then, that edited my article?" Khlopitz asks Svitlana Zhuravlynchenko as he reaches over for a pencil and makes a few marks on the page.

Ophelia Feliksivna raises her eyebrows, then her heels, and looks over at the page. Pencil lines, nothing more. Crooked, almost parallel lines.

"Me?!"

Everyone who looks up at the sound of this squeal of

Svitlana's watches someone invisible pour a flask of red ink over her face from behind.

"Looking for mistakes in my work again, Hryhory Davydovych?!"

"Me?!"

Khlopitz turns pale, as though he were not the leading scholar of a research institute but a three-liter jug of bluish milk from the corner store.

"When? Who? Me? I . . . "

All of Room 507 puts aside translation, editing, and internal life, and stares at Khlopitz in disbelief.

"Ha-ha-ha!" He regains composure and adds a little Mercurochrome to the milk. "Well, in that case, tell me, why do you make two paragraphs in place of my one? Why do you break up the flow of ideas?"

"You just can't do without nitpicking, can you, Hrysha," says Ophelia Feliksivna.

"The minute a woman's hand cuts through consistent logical thought," Khlopitz explains, "it immediately brings about the onset of what I call acausal synchronicity."

Khlopitz has abandoned drawing lines and switched to lightning rods and harpoons. He has a doctorate in the technical sciences, is interested in psychology, and does pastel drawings in his spare time.

"And Kraplysty, too, by the way! . . . " Ophelia Feliksivna once again jars her telephone friend in order to lash her subordinate, bypassing Khlopitz's head. "Kraplysty complained to me a while ago that you, Svitlana, put extra commas all over his project!"

The unjust insult helps Svitlana lose some color.

"That Kraplysty of yours doesn't have a clue about the elementary rules of punctuation in subordinate clauses!"

"Ha, ha, Ophelia!" Khlopitz discovers a way out. "See how easy it is to pull your leg! In fact, I came down here to personally thank your department and Svetochka in particular."

"Thank us?!" The Creator did not skimp on height with

Ophelia Feliksivna (plus the heels, plus the glasses), and she can see very clearly who's doing what and who's got what on his mind. Vitya Maliatko is chewing on his nail, Antonina Pavlivna is correcting something, Zoyka Vereshchak's eyes are flashing, Svitlana is blushing and passing out, and Khlopitz has come here to flirt!

"And what is it you want to thank us for?" she asks him.

"For the Sisyphean struggle with the word!" replies Khlopitz.

He kisses the fingertips of Ophelia Feliksivna's hand. She smiles. Before NIIAA, they used to work together in NIIUP.

"Hand me your complaints book," Khlopitz continues the banter.

Ophelia Feliksivna is pleased with the joke, but remembers why he wandered in here in the first place.

"You, Hryhory," she jests in return, "don't distract my girls from their work."

Khlopitz pulls his hands back, bows comically, and pauses only when he gets to the door to pronounce how anxiously he awaits the moment when the next brilliant invention of his section will come in contact with the gentle hands of these merciless censors.

"Out with you, out with you!" Ophelia Feliksivna waves him on. "Monsieur, monsieur! Just wait till I call Naomi!"

"He's . . . completely bonkers over her," Zoyka mulls things over. "Svetka, Svetka, well, how about that! . . . "

"Svitlana!" Ophelia Feliksivna raises her hand, pretending to give Svitlana a beating for stylistic negligence, but the latter jumps up, screams, "Just look at what he did here, he's destroyed a page of the director's article, the vandal, I'm going to go catch him and give him a piece of my mind right now, he can retype the whole thing this minute, and what is this anyway, I swear to God!" and runs out of the room.

She's not gone for long.

AND, TURNING DEEP PURPLE, ADDS: "IF NOT WITH HIM, then with whom?"

Svitlana married Vitaly Zhuravlynchenko for love. And everything was fine with them, except for one thing. Svitlana felt no sexual satisfaction. It did happen on a superficial level occasionally and only at the beginning, but as for complete, physical, with convulsive moans, spasms, floods of intense sensation, and loss of consciousness—never. Neither before marriage nor since. Before Vitaly she had sex with one man, a fellow in her class called Hennady. They went out for three months until Hennady dropped her for Maryna.

After little Dima was born they practiced coitus interruptus at Svitlana's request. Vitaly warned her that ejaculation could occur before he was able to cut short the sexual act. As a result, the act was drawn out to fifteen minutes while sexual excitement began to fall off, even without ejaculation. This worried Vitaly. Maintaining a state of expectation led to the almost total disappearance of ejaculation, regardless of the length of the act. With masturbation, however, the indicators were completely normal.

Vitaly became nervous, his sex drive waned, his erection fell, his sperm was either discharged prematurely or, conversely, could, in the midst of intense motion, display complete apathy. In order to check things out, Vitaly frequently entered into intimate contact with women during business trips. After one such episode, his casual acquaintance asked if he happened to be ill with syphilis. Vitaly responded in the negative, but then thought to himself: Why is she asking me about such a thing? Is it not, perhaps, because she herself carries inside her the bacilli of an incurable disease?

He submitted his blood to the Wassermann test four times, and the results came back negative every time. But this did not allay Vitaly's fears, because there were still gonorrhea, and trichomoniasis, and yeast out there. Defying all logic and common sense, his state of health deteriorated. Svitlana took him to see Dr. Umansky.

He told Vitalik: "You are a patient of medium height, your sexual organs fall within the norm. The urological examination did not reveal distinct irregularities. On the neurological side, a heightened reflex action of the tendons was noted as well as a slight tremor of the outstretched fingers."

Umansky asked many questions about their personal life, and then pronounced his diagnosis.

"You," he says to Vitalik, "are completely healthy. I see no sign of sexual impotence. Your temporary inhibition of this function is a phobia, possibly a reaction to your wife's coldness. I recommend sports, showers, ginseng, and powdered deer antlers. Your wife should drink hormonal solutions. I'm allowing you to sleep together. At the beginning of each sexual act, set the timer. According to the Vasylenko tables, duration of coitus fluctuates between one minute fourteen seconds (at 68 thrusts) and three minutes thirty-four seconds (or 270 thrusts). Let me know about any deviations from the norm. You can get my office hours at the reception desk.

"And you," he says, turning to Svitlana, "are a completely frigid personality. You have never developed a truly strong capacity for arousal, no matter what the duration of intercourse. Proof of this is the fact that you did not experience orgasm even prior to marriage. Although it's true that according to the data gathered by Wolfram, persistent anorgasmy can be observed in 40 percent of French women. And of two hundred pregnant English women, 1 percent doesn't know what sexual satisfaction is. Not to mention Vienna. About a third of the women there haven't the foggiest notion about orgasm, although 65 percent of them have had direct contact with various men. In a word, the situation with Vitalik is a direct result of your behavior and can lead to the destruction of the family."

"Oh!" Svitlana can feel her face burn.

"But," Umansky softens his verdict, "at the same time I can see that you are healthy woman in full bloom, eager to engage with others, sensitive, kind, self-confident, generous, with nicely defined secondary sex characteristics. We are obviously dealing here with a case of repression in the sexual sphere resulting from psychological trauma or an unsuccessful first experience. We will need to do a gynecological examination."

"Maybe it's not necessary?" she pleads.

"Lie down here!" commands the doctor.

During the examination intensive rhythmical pressure is applied to the G-spot in the frontal wall of the vagina. This induces an obvious erotic response on the level of reflex. A certain sensitivity is also elicited from the clitoris. The patient is impressed. First time in eight years of marriage!

"Stimulation," advises Dr. Umansky, "as much vigorous stimulation as possible."

"But what if even that doesn't help?" ask Svitlana Zhuravlynchenko.

"Then simulate," the doctor counsels. "And do not rule out masturbation. Modern medicine is not opposed to that."

He scrubs his hands long and hard with a special brush while Vitaly agonizes, not knowing where to discreetly place the honorarium—a cellophane bag containing chocolates and cognac.

At home Svitlana surrounds herself with the appropriate literature and goes to battle almost every night for Vitalik, for the family. But the more valiantly she performs her duty, the more actively she feigns consummate pleasure, the more miserable their lives become. Feelings of irrepressible hatred for Vitaly emerge and gain in strength. He, too, is trying his best, but when Svitlana hands him a manual on stimulation techniques he acts hurt, becomes withdrawn, sleeps on the floor, avoids physical contact, does not sleep at home for several nights in a row.

Not long afterward, he made the acquaintance of a rather loose young woman and under her active influence entered into sexual relations with her. It was then that he discovered his potential to be surprisingly high. This inspired him to repeated sexual performances without any stimulation on her part whatsoever.

Svitlana loses faith in herself, wants to get divorced and commit suicide. Why is it, she asks herself, that some women manage to experience orgasm three to five, or even fifteen, times by the time their husbands culminate their sexual act, and other women not once? And why did I happen to fall precisely into the second category? Oh, damned inequality! Patriarchy wherever you turn! They get everything! How am I to break out of this enchanted circle?

The book on sexual neuroses describes one interesting case. A woman was frigid for a very long time. She had come to detest her husband completely. Then, suddenly, in the middle of their marriage, she fell in love with a freight handler from their heavy-industry complex. But she hid her feelings. At night, in the middle of the act with her legal partner, she imagined the freight handler eagerly caressing her, and that image immediately caused her to experience hitherto-unknown pleasure. After that, orgasm began overtake her on a regular basis by about the third minute of each sexual encounter. She even fell in love with her husband.

"Will I, too, someday be able," Svitlana ardently asks herself, "to tumble headfirst into that which can neither be named nor adequately described?"

Her heart shriveled, waiting for some meager yet affirmative answer. That is why the first time Khlopitz called for her on the telephone and hung up, she understood: This is it! It's a crime to let chance like this go by. She has no right to do that. For her own sake. For the sake of her full self-expression. Her self-realization. For the sake of the family. For Vitalik. In order to break through to the zone of orgasm, even if it is with Khlopitz's help. And pull Vitalik over there afterward as well.

"Yes, I've done all I could," she confesses. "But now I have matured for a different life, full-blooded and real. I've suffered for it, I've dreamed for it, I've earned it."

So That Finally, on a Bed of Magnolias with Music Softly Playing, She Can Come Face to Face with Khlopitz

Ah yes, he saunters in slowly. Accompanied by his exquisite, arousing, uniquely individual scent, his perfectly manicured nails, his firm, at times supple, yet always masculine nose, his steady pulse, which at climax delivers 190 throbs per minute, his sculpted muscles, his stimulating clothing, woven from delicate shades and natural accents. His senses are always keen. He inhales the air and knows exactly when the betel leaves that his love rubbed down her body with were plucked. He feels the breathing of the stars, the density of ripened plasma, the pressure of a hot vowel long before That which has no name begins to rumble, ignite, and drive to a frenzy That the name of which cannot be spoken. For it is ubiquitous and for all time. He is not about to, for reasons of petty ego, rush the love instinct over the nearest precipice. Oh, no! He waits for the new moon, and then with taboo words, kisses, and tender strokes, slowly begins to prepare his chosen one for the fiery embraces, the biting of lips, the scratching of cheeks, back, and buttocks. And how expertly—gently at first, then with greater resolve—he fondles her mounds, reaching out with his tongue for the bud, wanting to suck it in, bite it, squeeze it, drink it down. Only to leave and slip down the crooked path into the valley, find a little well overgrown with bushes, clear the entrance in two or three brisk movements, and feel the young delicate shoot beat and vibrate. He'll play with it, allowing the moistened petals to open up, and he will find himself one on one with the *source*. But he is not one to pound at the door and, stumbling over the entrance, choke on his momentary pleasure. Oh, no! He's in no hurry. He'll lie back, hug her tightly, take a minute to catch his breath, check to make sure that he is eagerly awaited, and only then, removing all superfluous clothing, will he enter the warm house. At one-quarter power, half, three-quarters, and only then—full speed ahead. Three quick thrusts, pause. Then four, and he is still again. Three more, then on and up to ten, followed by one, but very powerful. With purpose. With passion. With hope. Twenty minutes at a time at first, then thirty-four, and finally a full twenty-four hours, on the beach, music playing, reading a harmonious book, never having removed his garments completely. The second day is to be greeted without clothing and filled to the brim with laughter. Let them each ride the other to their hearts' content, let passion get the better of tenderness. The sunset is to be met in the entwined languorous pose of a liana, wordlessly feigning tedium. On the third day of union—in the morning, at noon, and at dusk—the lovers prepare for the midnight fireworks with renewed vigor. They partake of the full palate of bold gestures and unexperienced positions, revealing hitherto-submerged talents, and engage in pastel discourse on artistic themes under the eucalyptus. Technique as you will. Tempo at your discretion.

And now the moment of final onslaught has arrived. All previous life has been mere preparation for this. Svitlana is nervous. This is no joke. Will she get there? Will she find it in herself? And what will she do with this knowledge afterward? And, more important, with whom?

"Ah!" she cries out, and tumbles into the embraces of Khlopitz. They race ahead to their common purpose, and in the end, synchronically, step in step, cry in cry, and gasp in gasp, burst through the exquisite barrier.

However, that which Svitlana sees on the other side does

not coincide in the least with the parameters of her fantasy. Instead of a soft, fragrant bubble bath with fancy foreign designs, she encounters the breath and the throb of sheer power.

Svitlana shuts her eyes, thinking that she has died. But she is mistaken. There is no death here, just as there is no division into familiar categories. There is neither "I" nor "It," life nor death, well-deserved satisfaction nor payment for the latter. And if you were to ask her at this moment, "Svitlana, what or whom do you see there?" she would open her beautiful but at this moment terrified and fascinated eyes even wider and would not be able to utter a word.

And if you were to say to her, "Fine, you don't want to talk, you don't have to. But at least give us a hint. What's going on out there?" the answer would still be the same.

"It just is!" a smart-ass might say in her place, but they aren't allowed in here. While Svitlana was so honored. For she was chosen by Khlopitz himself. But he, evidently, got carried away and took her a little higher than was requested. Not for long, mind you, but long enough for her to forget all about the fulfillment of her potential and maximal self-expression. Because here you must either dissolve and be all things at once or hide behind something trite and with shadow.

"Well," Khlopitz asks her, "will you be staying? Or what? I believe it was you that requested an orgasm? This is it—ecstasy. So, which will it be: here or there? It's up to you!"

"Make a Choice! Hurry Up! Yes or No?" Each of the Five Hears, Stunned by Their Unexpected Adventures

THAT'S EASY TO SAY: "DECIDE." THEY ALL SQUIRM.

Each has good reason to suspect that he or she has just witnessed a miracle (how else could you explain all this?), and yet not one of them is sparkling with iridescent joy.

And, truthfully, who in their place, having experienced such a thing, could avoid breaking out in a cold sweat and a severe case of the shakes? Who? Not Zoyka, at any rate. She burrows deep into her threadbare coat, wraps the scarf tightly around her several times, and prepares to suffocate at any moment, since wadding does not anticipate the free flow of oxygen.

Ophelia Feliksivna resembles a pillar of salt or, one should say, marble, since her skin is renowned for its whiteness even under normal conditions.

Vitya Maliatko, too, sits with his eyes protruding. His mouth is agape, and he wants to shout out something very profound, but the message has gotten stuck in his throat and is making him bulge out like a balloon.

Antonina Pavlivna is not in the habit of making a fuss in public even when racked, as she is this moment, by a tremendous pain, one far greater than the neat and only slightly peccable body in which it has lodged and is now harrowing mercilessly.

Svitlana Zhuravlynchenko's posture, on the other hand, is more difficult to define. Her eyes are closed, her limbs hang limply by her sides, and her breathing is far too fervent for an office environment. But if you were to look more closely, you would have to compare her with the sailor who was, once upon a time, for certain transgressions, tied to a mast and thrown into the ocean. He is falling headfirst into the black beyond, ready to leave this earth without a trace, but at the last minute, out of the blue, he is pierced by a strange excitement. Terror at first. But then exhilaration. Then vice versa. All mixed up. Because, of course, there is the black hole ahead. But at the same time, what a grand beginning! Something like this has already been portrayed in literature.

Nonetheless, even in this agitated state, pinned to the wall by difficult choices, the people of Room 507 attempt to think rationally.

We must examine this carefully, they say to themselves. There's no need to panic. What is this "yes or no?" Let's be specific. First look at the "yes." Drop everything. Run off somewhere. All of a sudden. Just take off. That's easy for them to say. But the outcome is what? If you look at it concretely? As if! No way! Someday, something, somewhere . . . Sure. Once upon a time. So there was an exchange of views. As a result of which a proposition was made. Yes. In general terms. But where's the guarantee? And a few explanations, please. Some plain and simple ones. Something that doesn't look like a dream. A hallucination. No, I'm not opposed to it! Who am I to argue? Or me? Or me? Who would do that? No, no, not at all! Although, on the other hand, why not? Where is it written? Who said so? Don't I have a right? Quite the contrary. Regardless of what's behind this. Or what it means. Let's be realistic, for once in our lives. Yes, certainly. Freedom. Let's assume that's correct. Creativity. Who could be against that?! So it would seem. Fine. Just for a minute. Let's visualize. Who's opposed? Me? No! Or, rather . . .

And what if you choose "no"? Don't touch anything. Leave everything as is. Just in your mind, for now. I have the legal right. Who's going to stop me? But, on the other hand, this is a sign! A hint. And it's addressed to me specifically. A warning. A chance. A gift. The last hope. A command. And punishment for not complying . . . Death, after a long incurable illness. With hellish pain. The torments of our children. Cancer. Paralysis. A hungry young body and a complete inability to love. Blindness that will stamp out an artistic destiny once and for all. Homelessness. Life on the street. "And what did you think?" they'll say. "We offered. And you spit upon us. You're in for it now!"

But you show a little understanding, too. Yes or no—this is something that still needs to be properly thought out. Let's assume I make a certain choice. It's not impossible. And then what? Where's the guarantee? The chances of success? We don't live out in the tundra, you know. And besides, there is such a thing as extenuating circumstances. Who's going to take them into account? There's only one way out, and that's to find another way out. Fortunately, there is a third way of voting. Abstention. Nobody's done away with it yet, to the best of our knowledge. Yes, no, abstain. Please announce that I've chosen "abstain." And legally table the motion for another time. What can I say, if you really want the honest truth, deep down I'm all for it, a "yes." But it's not something that can't wait. Objectively speaking. Another time. Take it easy! What the hell's the big hurry anyway? It's always better to be cautious. Screw it! I don't need this! Get out!

"Well? Yes or No? I'm Asking for the Last Time!" Thunders the Voice

ALL PRESENT HAVE DRAWN IN THEIR SHOULDERS AND AWAIT the worst. No one gets out alive. This is it—the moment of reckoning. If not now, then the next time you inhale. If not when you inhale, then when you exhale. Air cautiously enters the nostrils, gropes the walls, not being in any hurry to go deeper, and quickly gets the hell out.

But the earth doesn't part, the sky doesn't fall, subterranean gases don't explode, and serpents don't start pushing their way out of all the cracks. That which mere words cannot describe had appeared without warning and quietly vanished.

"Don't tell me it's over?" The folks can't believe their luck. However, rather than feeling relief (of course, nobody even dreams of things like peace of mind or a minimal standard of living!), everyone is struck by an awesome terror. Unshakable, endless, boundless.

Not the one referred to as "staring into the jaws of the

beast" or "hatred rearing its ugly head." If only it were that! Because "head" and "beast" means that you have come up to it, stretched out your hand in friendship, and it, the wretched thing, has crushed your extremity so mercilessly that all your joints are crackling. Or else it has shoved a dead frog into your hand. Or hidden a thorn or needle laced with poison between its fingers just to stick it into your eager palm. There have even been odious creatures who would first cough up something into their hand or smear it with excrement just to do something nasty to you.

But not in this case. You say "great" and extend your hand. But there's no one and nothing out there. A void. Silence. Who do you lean on? Whose ugly mug do you spit at? No rules, no prohibitions. They could at least have left some tiny, barely discernible point or dividing line in the remote case that something creeps up from behind your back and sinks its claws into your eyes, your Adam's apple, your armpit (or into that very same back, for that matter!), and there isn't anyone on hand to defend you.

Hey, everyone protests, this wasn't part of the deal! If we had only known or had a chance to peek into the future, if you had at least given us a hint of what it would be like . . . Well, then we would . . .

"Tamara Zhakarivna Wouldn't Be In Here By Any Chance?"
An Unexpected Guest Hails from the Doorway. It's
Rozzhestvenik, Chief of the ERA Machine.

EVERYBODY BEGINS TO FEEL NAUSEOUS. NOT BECAUSE IVAN Havrylovych is a son of bitch, boor, dirty old man, stool pigeon, and, as everyone had felt even this morning, the main item expelled daily from the System's digestive tract. It was, rather, because, when the doors opened and Rozzhestvenik's erect torso sprang into view, they all understood that this was the future. As requested. Not exactly their own—a bit of someone else's, it seems, was foisted on them accidentally, or perhaps deliberately. Someone had shrewdly calculated that no one would run to complain about such a glaring discrepancy.

In this future, the events of the last few years have had such an impact on Rozzhestvenik that the Soviet true believer takes up naturopathic medicine, eats granola by the fistful, and gargles with oil for half an hour every night before bedtime. He then veers sharply in the direction of horoscopes, flying saucers, the Himalayas, and the treatment of all illnesses with urine. When the Powers That Be announce an easing of restrictions on foreign travel, Rozzhestvenik buys two tickets, takes his son, and heads for the common grave of his father, a hero of the 1944 storming of the watery bulwarks of the Danube.

On the train he meets passengers emigrating to the state of Israel. After the second bottle, Rozzhestvenik admits to them that his wife, who is presently in a psychiatric hospital, is also Jewish and has relatives in the ancient homeland. "Then come on with us!" his new friends propose. "Pal, it's heaven down there!"

In Budapest they lead him to the immigration bureau. The bureau takes up the cause of reuniting him with his wife's relatives. The only thing lacking is his wife's permission, since their son is still a minor.

Rozzhestvenik calls home. He's lucky, his wife picks up the phone. She was just released from the Pavlov Psychiatric Hospital that day so she could come home and take a bath.

"Where are you?" She can't seem to grasp. "What permission? What's this about Israel?"

"If you don't do it, I'll hang myself! And I'll kill our son!" Rozzhestvenik promises, and so she gives him permission.

When his mother-in-law in Israel (already saddled with two daughters from her first marriage) sees the Cossack Rozzhestvenik against a backdrop of palm trees, she raises a veritable *gevalt,* gets on the blower to the asylum, and demands that her youngest darling take these two morons away immediately. And so, after several months, Rozzhestvenik manages to beg, borrow, and steal enough shekels from somewhere to buy tickets, and he and his son arrive at Mineralnye Vody, Russian Federation.

At customs they ask him who he is and why he doesn't have a visa. "Look here, it says Hungary. And this flight's coming from where?"

Rozzhestvenik explains everything to the major, just exactly as it happened. The major arrests him, holds him under lock and key for three days, then puts him on a train home.

That day Rozzhestvenik comes to work and falls at Director Mudrava's feet. "I can't," says Mudrava. "You really let us down."

Rozzhestvenik's wife, on the other hand, beats him less violently than usual (the reason he left her in the first place was her insane jealousy). She escapes from the hospital and says to him, "Let's go!" Rozzhestvenik spun a few times around the Ouija board, talked to the crystals, made up the horoscope charts, chewed on some granola, drank it all down with urine, and said, "Okay!" But then suddenly a tumor is discovered on his brain. The doctors say, "Surgery without delay!" He agrees. The operation is successful. But after a while the tumor returns, pressing against the scalp, forcing its way through the bony plate. The pain is unbearable.

Rozzhestvenik can't sleep. He remembers how he once served on the Kurile Islands. Conditions were tough, with the border right next door and nothing but goddamn water no matter which way you turned. And a strong wind blowing off the Pacific, dispersing the oxygen gathered by the glorious army drop by drop, bubble by bubble, with sweat and tears, so all Soviet people could breathe in peace for all time, and the fucking wind just kept sweeping it back into the billowing surf!

The next day he loses all feeling in his legs, his right arm, then his left, but his tongue still moves. Rozzhestvenik calls his son and tells him about a friend of his who had a visit from a relative, or was it an in-law, it doesn't matter, a millionaire from Canada. Our people, of course, put out a spread with everything they had, all homegrown: a little pork fat and something to wash it down with, a little onion, cabbage. The millionaire had one drink, then another, then quelled his awakened appetite as befits the occasion, and finally said: "If we ate this way back home, we'd squander our millions pretty quickly!"

Then the muscles of Rozzhestvenik's face gave out. And at the other end, no bowel movement for four days already. "What did I do to deserve this?" he asks. "I've always followed the party line! And should that disappear, I'd follow the new regime. Why have they abandoned me? Why won't anyone stretch out his hand, take me away? Or strangle me?"

His son got tired of nodding his head and began listening to subversive Western music through his headset. His wife is glued to the telephone.

"Close the windows!" whispers Rozzhestvenik. "We must increase our counterpropaganda immediately! We cannot lose our vigilance, our class bite. The Chinese Jew Mao Tsetung has raised his hand against Holy Mother Russia! Hey you! Anybody! Be a friend. Kill me. No! First give me a chance to live a little longer. But close the window. They got streetcars out there!"

"You haven't seen Tamara Zhakharivna, have you?" he changes his tone abruptly after dropping out of the future into our time.

The paralyzed listeners are struck dumb.

"I see!" Before leaving, he gropes the women and Vitya Maliatko with his sticky glance one last time, mumbles something, and melts into darkness of the corridor. They hear him shuffle past the elevator, pause in front of Room 505, and, evidently not catching a whiff of anything criminal, crawl back into his ERA room.

As for those whose fortune it was to glimpse the future, they are now of the opinion that it would have been better for them not to do that. Who knows what consequences this little adventure may have? Will there not be a price to pay? Some day in some way? In the meantime, each one of them draws instinctually toward the next person, reaches out for the warmth of his or her still-breathing body, seeks to find in it a touch of the sublime, yearns to love and to raise this feeling to a high aesthetic level.

Vitya Maliatko Can't Take His Eyes Off Antonina Pavlivna

HE TACKLES HER PROFILE ON THE COVER OF THE FOREIGN-currency volume. Rather common at first glance, it is, in fact, full of dignity. However, Vitya Maliatko knows from personal experience that a loathsome front view can sometimes be found hiding behind an attractive side angle, and so he takes the trouble of rising from his perch to study the face head on.

The front view does not disappoint him. A blond with full soft cheeks, a slightly longish nose (to be appreciated by a true connoisseur), and hair wound into a tidy roll at the back of the head. And a profound basic decency beneath which (he is convinced!) lie as-yet-undiscovered deposits of volcanic feeling.

Vitya Maliatko is swept up by sexual arousal as warm as the gulf wind. The pencil trembles and ruins an almost-finished portrait. But this is not a tragedy, for he has accomplished his mission, successfully returning Antonina Pavlivna back to her senses, and she, barely having torn out of her own reverie, rushes off to save Zoyka Vereshchak.

She walks up to her lair, pulls off her coat, her hat, her scarf, and, finally, digs out the half-conscious translator of

German texts. Zoyka reminds her of a small, frightened, defenseless animal. A hamster, a guinea pig, a mouse.

"A very nice girl, if you take the trouble to look!" She releases a flood of maternal warmth. "Modest, hardworking, and she's learned all those languages! If only she could find a young man. But nobody seems to notice her for some reason. Granted, a bit of that's her fault, too. You have to pay more attention to your appearance. Change your clothes more often. Make two or three more dresses. Buy another pair of pants. None in stock? Sew a pair. Can't get the fabric? But others manage to find it somehow. Same thing with the teeth. You don't have any gold? Get metal ones put in. And you must wash your hair more often. German shampoo gets rid of dandruff very nicely. Or you can get by with our Mykolayiv brand for the time being. A tube can last two months if you use it sparingly and only once a week. And if not, then for a ruble you can get a big bunch of burdock roots from the peasant women by the market. If you rinse your hair with burdock essence once a week and go on a special diet, the dandruff will vanish before you know it! But will she bother with it? Now, if someone were to come along who could recognize and value her spiritual qualities and then her physical ones as well! . . . And if he were to say to her: Don't you worry. I love and cherish and feel sorry for you very much. And no matter what happens I shall not leave you or let you freeze to death. From this day forth no one will ever pick on you again. And about that birthmark on your face that you think is too big, don't give it a second thought! Who doesn't have a few blemishes these days! I have one, too, but not on my face. In India birthmarks have been revered for centuries as a sign of great beauty. Women there have them implanted by the dozen. And I'll tell you something else. I'll tell you that after many years of searching I have finally found, under this corduroy smock, a pure and faithful heart. And now I will love you forever! To tell you the truth, I'm no movie star either. I put these glasses on back in day care and I haven't taken them off since. I have bit of a limp. But I am convinced that the more deeply and profoundly I immerse myself in your rich female spiritual life, the happier I'll be!"

"Oh!" Zoyka starts up, always ready to take flight, but then catches Antonina Pavlivna's gentle gaze and relaxes. And really, why jump at everything, when love and tenderness abound all around you?! She quickly absorbs the positive charges from the atmosphere in the room, but overdoes it as usual, and, to prevent herself from bursting, has to share the surplus warmth with the convulsed body of Svitlana.

"It's all right!" Zoyka consoles her. "Yes, it was the ultimate, sure, it was pleasure! And now it's gone! But it'll be back tomorrow. Is it really such a crime to lust after happiness? We weren't all meant to be housewives. Each of us must follow her own star. Svitlana is a WOMAN. Look at her figure, the curve of her eyebrows, her sense of the beautiful. She knows all the actors and which films they starred in better than anybody else, and she looks after the flowers in the room. Her eyes are deep. She knows all about cosmetic masks. And she doesn't mind sharing her secrets with her friends at work. She deserves a little luck, after all! Isn't life supposed to be that way, so that even if one individual suddenly finds some joy, the rest benefit, too? The total volume of goodwill increases, and everyone feels more content. That's true, isn't it?!"

Under pressure from these tender thoughts, the metal clamp that had gripped Svitlana unwillingly but ultimately releases her. Svitlana frees herself, sees a pale and motionless Ophelia Feliksivna to her left, and directs at her a wave of the affinity that has been carousing around the room for some time now. She chides herself for lack of self-control, calls herself stupid, irresponsible, urges herself to follow the example of Ophelia Feliksivna, who, as we know, has no lawfully wedded husband, but still leads a full, cultured life, goes to symphony concerts, to the opera, never misses the art exhibits that we get from Moscow.

Thanks to Svitlana, Ophelia Feliksivna emerges from her rigor mortis state without injury. Now only Vitya Maliatko sits unwashed by the communal outpouring of tender feelings. That's why he is the one Ophelia Feliksivna turns toward. Of course, she can see all his weird and wacky ways. He is often weak, superficial, impulsive. She knows he had a chance to escape, but couldn't do it. He was not able to become an artist, even a minor one, beginning with today. And that's why he's doomed. As are we all, in here. Weak, lonely, miserable. And that is why, she proceeds to convince herself, I must love him. And he must love me. In order to at least slightly alleviate our existence. Because we are all linked in one way or another. Each of us must realize that. Both the chosen ones and all the rest. Although I doubt that life will become easier for anyone because of it. All the same, may everything turn out the way it's meant to, sooner rather than later. As it is written. If these writings are preserved somewhere. If this really is love.

Who Knows How Much Longer Waves of Tenderness and Human Kindness Would Have Lapped Over Room 507 If Not for Woodnov's Telephone Call

HE ASKS OPHELIA FELIKSIVNA WHETHER VITYA MALIATKO IS at his desk (where else would he be, I can call him to the phone right now if you like) and then abruptly hangs up.

This action by the chief of the Foreign Contacts Group upsets the staff. What does he want from Vitya? Maybe it's not Vitya he's watching at all? What the hell would he need Vitya for, anyway, if you stop to think about it! It's the rest of us he's after! At the management's request. He's screwed a microphone into the receiver and now listens to every conversation. And all our thoughts. They say they've already come up with a gadget like that. On microchips, with amplifiers in your plasma. The Japs figured it out. And our Politburo purchased a floor model for an insane sum of money. So we can pirate it and produce our own brand in underground factories. First for outer space and then for the consumer market. So they can know everything about us. Let them! They can't fire everybody.

And thus with one senseless phone call everything falls back to the usual office routine. (Well, what's the big deal, Woodnov was probably butting out his cigarette in the ashtray and accidentally pressed the button with his elbow.)

The Liahushenko departmental report bobs up again somewhere on the horizon. The editors glance at each other. Can we polish it off in an hour?

The women rustle their pages, protecting themselves as best they can from a deluge of guests—Draznov from the Komsomol Youth Committee (dropped by to tell Vitya Maliatko that the reports and elections meeting is on Friday), Alik Dudka (looking for Rozzhestvenik), the draftswoman (everyone promptly forgot why she came by), and the nameless graduate student seeking the truth about current guidelines for the acceptance of dissertations: Is relevance, innovation, purpose, and practical application of the research paper the way to go, or should he, on the contrary, put methodology and thesis first, with supporting argumentation to follow later?

A powerful force is preventing the editors from a timely disposal of their task.

"We have to, girls, we have to!" Ophelia Feliksivna urges them on. "There's only an hour left. How many pages have you done? We'll all attack it full force. Whoever finishes first can help the others. Let's give it all we've got. And half an hour later—chip-chop—we can hand it in and forget about it. Quickly. Expertly. As a team."

"Who needs this anyway?" the girls snarl back. "You know as well as we do that this stuff isn't going anywhere. They'll come down with another order. You'll see. Tomorrow the director will get a call from the ministry saying they don't need it anymore. Or they'll postpone it till next week. Or forget about it. Or lose it. It wouldn't be the first time! You're talking as if this were your first year working here."

"For your information, I have been working here longer than any of you!" It doesn't take Ophelia Feliksivna long to assemble the clouds of hurricane rage. "More than any one of you put together! But for me, strange as it may seem, there also exists such a thing as ethics. And profoundly moral behavior. Without which self-respect is impossible. Yes, it's hard for me, too. Harder, by the way, than it is for you. The whole section rests on my shoulders. Stress inside me and nonsense all around. But one must live and one must struggle. Generally and, in this instance, specifically. And not because the Liahushenko report will rise to represent the department and the institute. No! It represents me as well. As a professional. As a person. And that is why I must and I shall fulfill my duty under all circumstances and under any management!"

No one is looking at his or her neighbor; each has buried himself in a putrid mound of dead words and is poking around in there.

Forty-seven minutes before the end of the working day, Tamara Zakharivna Lupova reminds them of her existence.

"How's the Liahushenko going?" she inquires through the telephone receiver. "Have you finished?"

"Almost done," reports Ophelia Feliksivna. "We've literally got . . . "

"Good. But give it a little rest. Put it aside."

"How? Who said? Why?"

"Liahushenko is to be put aside."

"But we . . . There's only about . . . Literally, two or three . . . "

"Get back to the annual report," Lupova explains. "The most important thing now is the director's papers. Right away. We've just had a meeting. We'll revise them a bit, and it's all got to be in the ministry tomorrow or the day after at the latest. They've announced an interregional competition. How much can you get done today? All right then, I don't want you pausing for a minute."

The editors silently shove the unfinished Liahushenko out of sight.

"I wonder what's happening with Andriy?" Antonina Pavlivna meanders to the phone on borrowed legs. Busy signals at the other end. She returns, pulls out the epic novel, opens it at random, and discovers that it's been ohh-ho-ho so many months since Streltsov's brigade has been holed up in the bush.

At first the going was rough, but then the wounds healed. Discipline went to the dogs. Because, naturally, one's got a pack of kids, another snores, this one likes to play Beethoven on the Jew's harp after dark (he's preparing for a concert, you see), that one's decided that she'd like to have plumbing installed rather than carry pails from the well. What could they do? Expand the already-available living space? With what? And where are you supposed to find the workforce?

Grant permission for each to dig out his own dwelling? Anywhere he pleases, perhaps, with whomever he pleases? That's all they're waiting for! Before you have time to blink an eye, they'll burrow here, furrow there, and turn the whole campground into shit! And what's more, they could conspire to dig a tunnel and escape. And then who's going to help you wage war on the gluttonous bourgeois peasantry? There's no end to the problems!

The commander and the commissar, the fierce revolutionary jerk Portanchuk, faced the question boldly and pondered it together all night long.

"You know, I dunn like it."

"As if I like it."

"Gotta finish the job!"

"How?"

"In one blow!"

"They'll survive anyhow!"

"So we'll gather everybody at the shooting gallery and announce . . . "

"Betta cock this size you won't! They'll feel it in their bones and take off in all directions, and then no way you'll flush 'em out again."

"We'll catch 'em by surprise! With dope!"

"What dope?"

"Ether, colognes, gasoline, the good stuff!"

"We guzzled all the good stuff for Communist Spirit Day!"

"Well, if this ain't a fucking son of a bitch! You sure there's nothing left? Maybe a drop of grease somewhere, or some glue, huh? Don't you grin at me, I can see right through you! I want everything down in the minutes!"

When Streltsov unglued his bleary eyes the following morning (they did, in fact, manage to find some glue the night before) and tried to go outside, he tripped and toppled a mysterious top hat that someone had left in the doorway, dousing the prostrate Portanchuk with something pungent-smelling and very much like ammonia.

Eagle-eye Zorkin tumbled into the dugout, all out of breath.

But Antonina Pavlivna doesn't have a chance to find out who was chasing him or what that column moving in the direction of the camp might be.

She Is Prevented from Doing So by the Rattle and Scrape of the Ancient Phone

"WELL, DID YOU GET THE GOOSE?" THE AUNT ASKS ZOYKA Vereshchak.

"No," admits Zoyka.

"Did you at least get a place in line?"

The niece is silent.

"I knew it," the aunt sighs. "I suppose I'll have to choke on the same old salad tonight. Drop off a couple of beets . . . I don't need potatoes . . . A half-kilo, no, a kilo of onions . . . You can get it all right here, at the vegetable stand on Twenty-fifth Anniversary of Reunification Street . . . You won't forget about the beets?"

"Why would I forget," replies Zoyka, "if that's the reason I'm going there?"

"Don't interrupt me while I'm thinking," snaps the aunt, "or I'll get all mixed up! You know how to make beet salad? You take a beet, wash it for a long time, but don't peel it, just like the potato, in separate pots. When it's all cooked . . . Just make sure you check it with a fork, because a knife can cut through a raw vegetable and you'll never know. Understand?"

"As if I've never made beet salad!" says Zoyka.

"Because potato salad," the aunt persists, "I mean, oh, what was that . . . beet! The other way around, that is! With potato you cut up some sausage at the very end, or else wieners. You can put meat in, too. But you ignored my request rather nicely, didn't you! Cute! Here I am sitting on the phone, dialing like crazy, and the super's wife is bellowing like a madwoman: 'Pervomayivna! Hey, Pervomayivna! They're selling geese out there!'"

"Incidentally," Zoyka puts her in her place, "I'm not exactly partying here . . . "

"Okay, that's enough, that's enough," the aunt barely has enough time to say before hanging up. "You just, you know

. . . beets, onions, peas, too, if they're in glass jars. But no cans, you hear? They put some kind of strange smell in them. And come on over. You're only sitting around and wasting time there."

Zoyka prepares to drown herself in tears, but is distracted by a lively conversation her friends have started up so as not to waste time needlessly.

"Everyone always says: 'Pushkin! Pushkin!' But I'll tell you, I can understand his poor wife, Natalia Goncharova. He cheated on her, didn't he? He did! It's all proven. So what do you expect after something like that!"

Some embark on defending Natalia Goncharova's husband. Others condemn him.

"Have you heard that somewhere in the West they found the shroud Jesus Christ was buried in? And there was an outline of his face on it! They studied it with X rays and lasers in the labs for many years, and made a photograph of what they were able extract."

"So what does it look like?"

"Kind of blurry. Look at all the years that have gone by, but you can still make out a few features. A man. With a beard. Thin. Aquiline nose. Jewish."

"Jesus? Jewish? Are you serious?!"

"Well, what did you think?! Jesus was Jewish. It's been proven. And the Bible says so, too."

"But only one parent."

"So what? It all goes by the mother with them."

Antonina Pavlivna suddenly remembers Ophelia Feliksivna and turns red.

"Now, how can you say something like that!" Svitlana Zhuravlynchenko rushes to the defense of both Antonina Pavlivna and Ophelia Feliksivna. "Christ was . . . He, well . . . What do you call them . . . a convert!"

The telephone calls out. Svitlana Zhuravlynchenko's husband Vitaly has phoned to say that he'll be working late and can't pick up Dima.

"Aah!" Zoyka suddenly says. "I wish I could fly!"

Vitya Maliatko reminds her of Maksim Gorky's famous aphorism that those born to crawl cannot fly.

"When did I ever crawl?" Zoyka cries out, shocked by such cynicism.

"Hey, Zoy, uh Zoy!" the women distract her. "Look who's come to see you. No, not there! Turn around! Toma's calling you!"

"Cummeer, gotta tell you something," whispers Toma. Disheveled Zoyka dives through the crack of the door.

"Did you notice," says Ophelia Feliksivna, "that Toma didn't say hello again?!"

"Oh, Ophelia Feliksivna," they tell her, "leave her alone."

"She's rude," answers Ophelia Feliksivna.

"What does she want from our Zoy?" Antonina Pavlivna wonders.

"We'll find out soon enough," says Svitlana Zhuravlynchenko.

"If we're told," grimaces Ophelia Feliksivna.

"She'll have no choice," Vitya Maliatko assures her, and he is not mistaken.

Zoyka returns to say that Toma has just found out that it looks like the director has signed a document about the construction of a nine-story building for one- or two-person families. These would be primarily young specialists from NIIAA, NIIUP, and TSNIPIZU. There's a major battle going on right now, because HIDROFUKS is trying to muscle in on this as well, promising to make arrangements with the contractors and assist with finding a site. If you turn them down, they could sabotage the whole project. It seems as though Zoyka wasn't on the initial waiting list. But Toma wormed her way into Boozyn's good graces and managed to beg and plead him into opening up an additional supplementary reserve list in the event that someone refuses, is fired, or dies. He placed Zoyka Vereshchak first on that list. Now we have to wait until they excavate the site and divide the waiting lists into brigades, so they can work on construction Saturdays, Sundays, and sometimes even weeknights. Living space will be assigned according to the number of workdays you put in. Regular Volunteer Saturdays for the institute don't count. Overtime, night shifts, and bringing in assignments ahead of schedule do not increase time off. Shock brigade duty during state and revolutionary holidays does not count toward vacation time. Participation in construction is no guarantee of a housing assignment.

"So," says Vitya Maliatko, weary from a day of idleness, "when do we celebrate? Invite us for a housewarming!"

Today he hadn't translated a single word. His guilty conscience drives him to run over and hug Zoyka Vereshchak. The latter fights him off, squeals with delight, waves for Svitlana Zhuravlynchenko to come to her aid, calls Vitya a "dumbbell."

"Will you let me up to your balcony? You can tie two virgin-white sheets together . . . "

"Dumbbell!"

"What do you have there?" asks Vitya Maliatko and pokes his finger at Zoyka Vereshchak's chest. As she bends her head down, Vitya grabs her by the nose.

"Knucklehead," Zoyka shouts gleefully, "too bad I don't have a cold!"

"Hey there!" Svitlana Zhuravlynchenko joins the game. "Don't corrupt the child!"

"Girls," Vitya Maliatko hovers over Svitlana, "are you sisters?"

"Oh," quivers the merry widow Svitlana, "help me, Zoy! Zoy, help!"

At the sound of this tumult Agnesa Lucianivna rushes into the room, attired in a coat and fur hat. She assesses the situation pretty quickly.

"What's this," she asks "a ménage à trois?"

"Zoy's getting an apartment," they explain to her.

"Oh, stop! What are you talking about!" Zoyka eagerly flaps her arms.

"You know," says Agnesa Lucianivna, "during lunch break today someone tore down a portrait from the Employee of Honor board . . . you'll never guess whose . . . Krupsky's!"

"That'll be Vladimir Illich," Vitya Maliatko explains.

"Turkey!" Zoyka shoves an elbow into his ribs. "Viktor Viktorovych is a very distinguished gentleman, and you can keep your risky jokes to yourself . . . "

"It must be an inside job," Ophelia Feliksivna gives her assessment. "After all, he's been in charge of internal housing distribution in the trade union for the past three years. You can't please everybody. And, of course, our people are pigs."

"And anyway," says Agnesa Lucianivna, "it's beyond me why our management doesn't post the truly deserving on the honor board rather than one person from each department. For example, what if our department has two or three? Genuine yet modest and unassuming Stahkhnovites! And what if other departments, if you want to hear a little secret, have none?! Do you consider that fair?"

"Here I Am!" Marusyk Flings Open the Door Joyfully, and with This Adept Movement Focuses All Attention on Himself. "How Have You Been Without Me? Lonely? Bored?"

"AH, YOU HAVE NO IDEA, MAN!" THE WOMEN ALL RAISE THEIR arms. "We're dying in here! Rotting alive! No one to console us, no one to amuse us. You're like a ray of sunshine. Why do we see you so rarely? Where the hell have you been?"

"Hush, sweeties," Marusyk rubs his hands together with glee. "You know that I'd sacrifice my own father for you. But what can I offer, except my chains?"

"Oh, that's a good one!" cackle the sweeties. "As if your kind can be chained down!"

"But imagine this!" Marusyk persists. "I give you only one striking example. Right now we've got—what? 5:24 P.M.

What are your average NIIAA research associates doing this minute? Packing up their stuff! And what am I doing? Lifting up a certain body part, if you'll pardon the expression, heaving it all the way up to the fifth floor to the office of the esteemed translator Victor the Son-of-His-Father, whom, bowing deeply, I ask to translate a tiny little article on recent developments in cybernetics from one of the journals of our avowed ideological foes. You think I personally need all this? No, Lord, no! It's our dear institute I care about! The development of our national scientific and technical 'exportease'!"

Vitya Maliatko hastens to open the megavolume on quality and begins to explain to Marusyk why he will not be taking on this assignment. He suspects that Marusyk has already run over whining to Woodnov's and that the latter has undoubtedly promised to help eradicate the free spirit Vitya Maliatko from the face of the earth. If only Marusyk would help Woodnov collect enough weighty compromising material, preferably with concrete evidence . . .

And he is not mistaken. Marusyk has indeed met with the chief of the Foreign Contacts Group and has even played chess with him. Woodnov has received the message that translator Maliatko is depriving NIIAA of valuable scientific information from potential enemy sources, but has decided not to panic about it just yet. Rather, he inquires of Marusyk in detail about his work and about his dissertation, on account of which he wasted five years in graduate school (three legitimately, plus two on academic leave by virtue of falsified papers), and in the end successfully managed not to pass a single Ph.D. exam.

And then, incidentally, as it were, Woodnov looks deep into Marusyk's eyes and asks how he enjoyed working at the collective farm and with which members of the opposite sex was he able to bond more deeply, so to speak.

"What does this have to do with the fact that one of the colleagues entrusted to your care is not fulfilling his assigned duties?" Marusyk would like to know.

"I'll explain," Woodnov says to him. "The fact is that each of us has a family, which must serve as a strong link in the chain of our social order. Some of us have yet to understand that, and allow themselves to deviate to the left."

"In other words?" squirms Marusyk.

"In other words: June 16, State Farm Peresan, acacia woodland strip, 23:00 to 23:10 (that seemed to be as much you could muster that evening, according to my sources), Alla the typist . . . Shall I go on? Or perhaps pick up the phone and share this with your lawfully wedded, as they say, other half? She, uh, works over at NIIUP, if I'm not mistaken?"

"Who said? When? It's a lie!"

"Ah, if only, if only!" Woodnov is clearly pleased by the response. "The ladies have been complaining about you. You can't carry on this way, pal . . . And then you want us translate all kinds of nonsense for you. Why should we? What do we get out of you? It's not like you'll use it for the good and glory of the Motherland. It'll be for one of your shoddy schemes. You think I don't know you? You think all I've got on you is this one little item?"

In the end they agree that Woodnov will squeeze the translation out of Vitya Maliatko for Marusyk, and Marusyk will go to Room 507, talk to Vitya Maliatko once more, and simultaneously check out the mood among the ladies. Just in case they've been yapping some outrageous nonsense. Damned broads! Or maybe it's Vitya Maliatko that's been spreading the dirt. And if they want to play dirty, we can play dirty, too. We won't stand by and let the names of honest cadre be sullied! Those days are over! But it is important to know. About everybody. As much as possible. Ahead of time. You know yourself what I'm referring to . . . In the West they have technology for this sort of thing. Everywhere you look—in America, England, France, in the . . . oh, who the hell are they, uh . . . Netherlands, damn them! The boys told me. Even in our own godforsaken Hungary! Microphones all over the place, space-age equipment—science fiction! But here you're on your own, manual labor. A creative approach is your only hope.

"And if he dares tell me," predicts Marusyk, "'I can't, director's assignment, ministerial level, foreign-currency publication . . .'"

"Don't you fear nothin', my friend! What's he gonna do?" Woodnov promises. "I'll get the Komsomol league after him. We'll call a meeting. Get him to prepare a report on something. If he refuses, he gets an official personal reprimand. He's still a rookie. In foreign languages. With a chance of going abroad. That's the first thing. And if he decides to be an ass, I'll get the military draft involved. Let him serve a couple of years! Nobody gets away from me!"

"Director's Assignment!" Vitya Loads It On, as Expected. "Ministerial Level! Foreign-Currency Publication!"

"I UNDERSTAND," MARUSYK SAYS TO HIM, "BUT YOU SHOW A little understanding of my . . . "

"I'm always understanding as far as you're concerned. But sometime around the middle of next week," Vitya goes out to meet him halfway. "Just let me get caught up a bit . . . "

"Well, maybe we can do it this way," Marusyk projects. "I leave you the article today, and tomorrow you . . . "

"I'd love to help you," says Vitya Maliatko, "but . . . "

"Well, perhaps . . . "

"I swear it!"

"Oh, don't do this, please!"

"I swear by Jove!" says Vitya.

"There's no need for that," sighs Marusyk. "I could still see Neptune, Uranus, Pluto. But Jupiter . . . You're sure you won't regret it? By the way! I see that you're interested in philosophy. I've been promised a forbidden work by Nietzsche, *So Says Zlatoustra,* which, incidentally, Hitler really liked to read, because it predicts the future so well. What do you say? Interested?"

"Nice weather we're having today," answers Vitya Maliatko.

"I get it," says Marusyk. "Would you like me arrange for a special official thank you from our department? And have it noted in your employment record book? It won't be easy, but if I bring in all my underground channels . . ."

Svitlana Zhuravlynchenko takes the carafe with grayish-brown rings of ancient deposits and goes over to water the flowers and cactuses.

"Did you watch the show yesterday," she asks everyone, "you know, the one after the news? You should have seen them dance!"

"I'll tell you," Ophelia Feliksivna picks up the cue, "those Leningraders are just the best."

"What about Minsk?" they ask her.

"No way! How can you compare them?"

"But at least they make good refrigerators in Minsk," they tell her. "Not like ours . . ."

"But we," Zoyka speaks up, "we've got the greatest chestnuts! I was gathering them all through September and the middle of October. You know how good they are for fighting moths?!"

"What are you talking about!" retorts Svitlana. "Last year I put a package of rolling tobacco on every one of my ledges, but they still chewed right through it, and stinking with cigarette smoke, crawled on to gorge themselves on my holiday sweater. I bought it in a boutique two years ago for 128 rubles. Handmade!"

"Oh no!"

"Sure! Let me tell you, for them to settle into a package of tobacco is like, let's see, the same as for you or me to get a three-room apartment in, let's see, where? . . ."

"A foreign-currency store!"

"A candy store! The Communist Party sanatorium resort!

They get thirty different kinds of chocolates delivered there every day!"

"Why are you talking about a candy store?" Agnesa Lucianivna isn't following the conversation. "Since when do they sell tobacco in a candy store?"

"Real chocolate!" persists Zoyka. "Not the cheap stuff, not soya, but genuine World War II air force pilots' chocolate! In bars. Some people have it all!"

"Well? Have we agreed?" Marusyk moves in real close, and his mouth cuts off the air supply to both of Vitya's nostrils. Vitya collapses into a choking coughing fit. Marusyk jumps back, pulls out a hanky, and proceeds to wipe his face clean of Vitya's globules for some time afterward.

"How's your health?" Agnesa Lucianivna asks Ophelia Feliksivna.

"I'm so sick of it all!" she answers.

"I understand you so well!" Agnesa Lucianivna lowers her voice and looks around.

"I'm going to drag myself home and lie down," confesses Ophelia Feliksivna.

"Don't you dare!" Agnesa Lucianivna jumps up and lectures her friend in a powerful voice. "You have to walk!"

"How can I walk when I'm tired?"

"Movement is therapeutic."

"I walked and walked and look at what I've gotten myself into. Remember what condition I was in last week? Humanity pays dearly with its spine for the fact that it walks on two legs instead of four. And this is only the beginning!"

"Nonsense! All the theories will tell you that everybody has to keep moving all the time. Even the paralyzed."

"First I just walked around," Ophelia Feliksivna explains to her, "then I followed the fitness course routes, then I joined the health club. And so what did they say to me? They said, she's joined the health club—so she must be as healthy as an ox, she can go out and do her stint at the collective farms! Oh no! I'd rather crawl home as best I can, fall into bed, take some triasizirundin, and rest."

"Don't do this! Damn you!" Agnesa Lucianivna practically hurls herself at Ophelia Feliksivna with her fists.

"What are you saying?!" Ophelia Feliksivna fights off Agnesa Lucianivna. "If you had my allergies! . . . "

"Oh, you think I don't have allergies of my own?!" retorts Agnesa Lucianivna. "How dare you say that to me?! Do you want me to strip off my clothes and show you?! Oh, excuse me, there are men present."

"You call those men?" snorts Zoyka.

"What do you mean by that?" Marusyk, still splattered by Vitya, jumps up.

"Oh, I didn't mean you!" Zoyka shakes her fists merrily. "I was taking Vitya as a . . . !"

"And how exactly were you taking him, if I may ask?" Marusyk regains his cool.

"Way to go, Zoyka!" the women break into a friendly cackle.

"So," Agnesa Lucianivna carries on with her theme, "allergies and diatheses are my domain. I've tried everything from urine to Lorinden ointment on my own children!"

"Yes," Ophelia Feliksivna is using every last resource to control herself, "I am truly grateful to you. I even bow my head before your infinite wisdom! But I ask you, please, not to use your children as a weapon against me. In order to treat one's ailments it is not necessary to give birth or force someone to drink the by-products of one's own body. It is sufficient to read the reference literature."

"Don't think for a moment that I'm threatening you!" Marusyk puts away his handkerchief, nestles up to Vitya Maliatko, and douses him with a cloud of putrid rotting breath.

"What have I done to deserve this?" Vitya raises his eyes to the heavens. "Will it always be like this? Either sniff and enjoy, or sooner or later Marusyk's cavernous teeth will chew their way through your throat. They had it good in the old days! Some had serfs taking care of their needs. Another had his mother sending regular food shipments to Rome. Van Gogh got money from his brother. Marx got his from Engels. If only I had something like that! Every morning I would, like Adam, walk out of my cabin in the dense forest to the bank of the river, then race full speed and dive in against the current, feeling my blood disperse artistic images, the way a flute does. And in the evening, having absorbed the free vibrations, I'd put on jeans and a sweater, and wind my way through the backstreets to town to meet with friends, savor red wine, hurry to see a trusted woman."

"You See, My Friend, You Have to Do It! It's Frightfully Important! Desperately!" Marusyk Is Hugging Him Tightly

"I'M A FRIEND! YOU MUST UNDERSTAND THAT! AND IT'S MY duty to forewarn about what awaits you in this life. It's all decided up front. With no exceptions or variations. Forget your youthful hopes and dreams. A swamp rots for hundreds of years on end. And don't think for a moment that I'm threatening you. Oh no! All of my conscious life I have lived by the principle 'Don't say—do; don't threaten—strike!' And I must say, the results have been excellent. Let's take your example. I could get Lupova to see the light anytime I choose. Tamara, I'd say to her, old girl, what's this bordello of a department you're running here? Where, for God's sake, is your conscientious fulfillment of orders? Where is the sensitivity and respect for the needs of the technical elite on the part of humanities personnel? Your people are sabotaging our programs. And I wouldn't do it myself, I assure you, but through a telephone call coming from the top. This is elementary. I could cause some ver-ry serious trouble for certain people. And then there are other channels. From the District Police RVD to the Psychiatric PND, all the way to the good old KGB and the insane asylum. Woodnov's got a truckload of evidence against you just waiting to be used. Vitya-boy, it could be a nightmare. But I say to him: Listen boss, Vitya Maliatko is my buddy. You touch him and you'll have to deal with me. I positively do not advise you to do this. Moreover, I've already made arrangements with Maliatko. He's doing a translation for me. For tomorrow. And in exchange I'm going to make sure that he . . ."

"I'll be right back," says Vitya and runs out of the room.

No sooner does the door slam than Woodnov phones demanding to speak with Vitya Maliatko.

"Where's he off to so early?" he asks. "The working day isn't over for another fifteen minutes."

"I don't know," answers Svitlana Zhuravlynchenko. "His coat is still here. Is there a message . . . "

But Woodnov hangs up.

"This Maliatko of yours," Marusyk tells the ladies in the room once the poppy-red expression of surprise leaves his face, "is a very strange fellow. Does he often behave this way . . . ?"

Vitya's colleagues rush to his defense.

"Did I say anything?" Marusyk returns to joking. "For me it's strictly a matter of sociological interest. But how's his knowledge of the language? Has he ever been abroad?"

He is told that it's not absolutely necessary to go to a place to acquire command of a foreign language. It often happens that those who never go anywhere master a language to a far greater extent.

"That's very true," Marusyk agrees. "Although it wouldn't hurt to take a little trip somewhere for about a year or two. Is this correct what I think? . . . therefore I am?"

He manages to direct his wink at Svitlana Zhuravlynchenko as well as Ophelia Feliksivna and Agnesa Lucianivna simultaneously. The women don't notice the perfidy and complain to him about isolation on the international scene.

"And why is it like that?" Marusyk asks and answers his own question. "Because in our country everything is done without thinking about it first, very irrationally, ass backward. Let's take those notorious queues as an example. Do we have such a problem? Do we ever! But in France . . . "

"Found the perfect comparison!" the women burst out laughing.

"Why not?" Marusyk winks at Zoyka and Antonina Pavlivna. "Let's sit down right now and examine France! Their women don't run around from grocery store to grocery store, but walk into any bistro, fill up a huge bag, and there's a bill already added up and waiting for them at the cash register. Because the cash registers work at the speed of human walking!"

"Isn't a bistro the same thing as a café?" says Svitlana Zhuravlynchenko.

"Did I say I was opposed to that?" Marusyk looks over at her in surprise.

"Ah, Paris, Paris," sighs Ophelia Feliksivna.

"And it's like that everywhere now," says Marusyk, "not only in Paris, but even in godforsaken Hungary. I went over to Bulgaria last summer . . . What can I tell you . . . "

"Don't talk to me about Bulgaria!" Agnesa Lucianivna erupts. "Lucy Katolyk, who works in our department, they heisted twenty-five rubles from her purse! And in Syluyan's department it was a box of marshmallows! An inside job. I even have a pretty good idea . . . "

The telephone ring doesn't let her finish her thought.

"One moment!" answers Svitlana, and calls Antonina Pavlivna.

"What the Hell's Going On There?!" Volodya Shouts at His Faithful Wife

"WHY CAN'T I GET THROUGH FOR HALF A DAY? NO, EVERY-thing's fine with us. Nobody broke anything. Andriy, like an idiot, yanked the receiver and the phone hit the stool, but I caught it in time. No. Nobody called me. But I do want to talk to you about something else. Don't you ever kid around with me that way again. Because I could get upset. You know what could happen then? I think we've already had a conversation about . . . He doesn't have a fever. Don't change the subject. Do you understand what I'm getting at? He took a nap. No, he's not crying. That's the radio. In other words, if there are any more problems—you take sick leave. And the main thing is hurry home, we're starving. Doesn't matter. Whatever you get is fine. You're asking as if there's some big choice. Some kind of sausage, I don't know . . . Rusty nails, acetone. Just hurry up. Well, that's all, love you, gotta go, there's a good program coming on here. No. I told you, he's not sleeping, he's reading something. I warmed up some soup, but he doesn't want to eat. He's in his room. I'll call him. Aan-drei-us! Where are you? An-drei-otti!"

She can hear the door open, someone walking, and in the meantime a consummately objective baritone recites the evening news. Doors click, two different kinds of footsteps.

"I don't want any more!" whines Andriyko. "I'm not hungry."

"Sit down!" Volodya orders his son.

"I can't eat any more. Why did you interrupt me? You know what's in that book?"

"Eat!"

"I don't want any!"

"Eat, just do it quietly. I missed the name of that country because of you!"

"I didn't hear it either, but I think that the people won't

be able to benefit from this, because, as history teaches us, the ruling classes always . . . "

"All right, let me listen!"

Andriy stops talking so that in a minute he can shout out, "So that's where Vanavara is!"

"Who?"

"Faktoria Vanavara."

"You look at your plate, not the map. Everything's cold already."

"That's where the Tungus meteorite came down! It was several times brighter than the sun. One blind woman saw the taiga for the first and last time in her life that time!"

Ophelia Feliksivna is asking why Antonina Pavlivna is tying up the line for so long without saying anything. Antonina Pavlivna answers that Volodya is relating the doctor's instructions. She hasn't lost hope that her husband will notice the telephone receiver and remember her.

"Yes, yes!" She simulates a lively conversation.

"Dad, why does Dean Reed live in Berlin?"

"I don't know."

"Tablespoon or teaspoon?" she inquires about possible suggestions from the district doctor.

"When exactly did people start to worship Stalin?"

"Quiet, you! Let me listen to the news!"

"On an empty stomach or with food?" Antonina Pavlivna wants to know.

The radio crackles. Volodya fiddles with the bands.

"Dad, do they tell the truth or do they lie?"

"Who?"

"The radio."

"Eat!"

"Let's find out."

"How?"

"Let's write to them and ask."

"Who?"

"The radio. Or the newspaper. I noticed that people write and they answer all their questions."

"And what if the paper lies?"

"Why would it? You said yourself that the truth only brings good to people."

Ophelia Feliksivna has lost her patience. They could disconnect our telephone for these kinds of conversations!

"All right," sighs Antonina Pavlivna. "I'll be there soon, and you two be careful, make sure there are no drafts in the house."

She gingerly puts down the warm receiver, like a child into a crib.

Ophelia Feliksivna, having dislodged her colleague, gives Agnesa Lucianivna a chance to put a call through to her son and ask him how school went and what he warmed up his mutton and buckwheat in.

Thank God everything turned out all right, muses Antonina Pavlivna. If only I could get home soon. What can I make them for supper? I'll probably head down to the central market, it's open till seven, I'll get some nice meat and make chops tonight. Volodya will help me. And on the way I'll pop into the grocery. I'll make something for dessert. Cake. Pudding. I think there was some cheese left over. Unless Volodya ate it. What if he ate it? And what if they close the market at six and they haven't brought anything into the grocery? By the way, what are we going to do about sick leave? Volodya probably didn't think and said that we don't need it anymore. And what if Andriy's temperature suddenly goes up? How can I protect him from infections? Life is such a dangerous thing. What are you to do with it? Who can you count on? Only on yourself.

Under no circumstances, Ophelia Feliksivna decides for herself, should you suppress your natural reactions. Let your brain respond as it wishes to this savage external world. Let it issue the appropriate commands to the glands. Let them, in turn, release the hormones. Let the hormones plunge into the bloodstream and, having made their way through the labyrinth, return to the brain.

Svitlana Zhuravlynchenko agrees that our life is a dark dense forest, but she's a little afraid of relying on the body alone. Because here's a good example for you. She, for one, takes all possible precautions. She is so careful! . . . And still! Today, no matter which way you count, her period is a full seven days late. Don't say she's going to have to go to those backstreet butchers again?!

At this moment Zoyka Vereshchak is not thinking about survival. Her attention is now gripped not by the housing question, not by her aunt's beet salad, but by the born actor Marusyk. Having forgotten all about Woodnov's assignment, he is skillfully relating to Agnesa Lucianivna a joke that he heard on the third floor from the engineer Pryrechenko.

"Oh, girls!" Ophelia Feliksivna can't believe her eyes. "It's six! Whatever are you thinking?!"

The girls fold up, drawers slam. The crooked coatrack, now relieved of their coats, resembles an artificial limb.

"Just a minute!" Marusyk pokes his finger at the threadbare article that is Vitya Maliatko's garment.

And Where's This Baby?

THE WOMEN THINK. BUT THEY ARE IN NO HURRY TO ANSWER. He's not in the room, that's a fact. Where is he now? Maybe he got scared of Marusyk and is hiding out somewhere. It's not like he doesn't have any friends on the other floors! He could even be hiding in the attic. Everyone will leave, and then he'll make his way along the walls down to the lobby, calmly pick up the key, and come back to take his coat. Who's to stop him?

But it's not impossible that he, even if it was ten minutes before the end of the day, was actually able to break out to freedom. The only one of them. It would be him. Bypassing the lobby, through the basement bathroom, pushing out the window bars that had been sawed through earlier. In order to never come back here again. Maybe the conversation with Marusyk was the last straw. Maybe he even scraped himself against the metal rods and, in that first moment, when he breathed in the chilled air, regretted his action. For some time he shivered under the concrete NIIAA block, watched its yellowish cataracts disappear one after another at six o'clock, and hesitated. Should he burn his bridges or go back? Pretend it was all a joke, perhaps even repent? Or should he leave everything to them: his coat, his scarf, letters of recommendation, record of employment with ranking of professional hours, knitted hat—and rely solely on his own body, on the fact that blood warms up quickly when one runs wild, and then his creative juices will begin to flow, the pores will open, contact will be established with the higher spheres, and it will be possible to absorb their vibrations.

It's hard to say. And who can give the definitive answer? Sitting here. In Room 507. You can't see anything from here. In any case, the objective facts are that his coat is here and he is not.

Although, why not? It's quite possible. Knowing Vitya Maliatko. He gets something into his head and he does it. But to vouch that this is in fact the case and not the complete opposite, or give a guarantee . . . No. That's risky. It's a good thing that at least hope is still around.

The clock strikes six. They walk out together, earnestly speaking of poultry stuffing and children's diseases. Ophelia Feliksivna locks the door, turns out the light, and hangs up the key in the lobby.

1974–93